STRINGS ATTACHED

M. A. FRÉCHETTE

FOREWORD

A fledgling journalist. A masked killer. The scoop of the century, if she survives the interview...

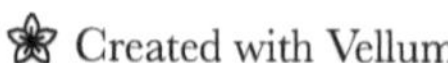 Created with Vellum

TRIGGER WARNINGS

- Sexually explicit scenes
- Anal sex
- Mention of past sexual assault
- Mention of past child abuse
- Blood and gore
- Talk of suicide
- Kidnapping
- Drug addiction
- Needles/injections
- Confinement
- Serial killer
- Stalking
- Home invasion
- Hidden camera
- Invasion of privacy
- Intended theft
- Murder
- Dismemberment
- Description of violent deaths
- Mention of cancer

- Death of parents/sibling
- Breath play
- Knife play
- Fear play
- Primal play
- Mask play
- Nipple play
- Rope play
- Whipping
- Somnophilia
- Consensual dubious consent

To my readers: Don't try this at home.

1
———

UNEXPECTED MEETING

A streak of sunlight hit the paper taped to the door, and as I approached, it heated my back. A message left instructions on a new location while the professor's office was being repaired—something about the air conditioner not working. I couldn't blame him; it would be impossible to work in this heat without some sort of cooling system. But still. We had an appointment scheduled, and he could've warned me before I walked clear across the campus for nothing in this scorcher.

I pulled out my phone and took a quick photo of the note in case I needed it for reference later. Plus, the phone number he'd left behind might come in handy if I ever ended up being late. Not that he could blame me since he was the one who'd moved without a single notice. Except for this paper taped to the door.

I put my cellphone back into my messenger bag and adjusted the straps of my sundress and bra for the hundredth time that day; it wasn't the most comfortable piece of clothing I owned, but it was the lightest material I had.

The small agenda the university provided came in useful as I looked at the campus map, trying to find the new location of Professor Frauley's temporary office.

"Oh, that's fucking great," I muttered when my finger landed on the other side of the map. And because it was located in the old houses bought out by the university to make more offices, there was no way to get to it by walking inside the buildings. Instead, I had to leave the cool air and walk outside through Satan's ass crack to get there.

I could already feel the chaffing of my inner thighs despite wearing shorts; they rode up constantly, and having to stop every few minutes to yank them back down was annoying for more than a few reasons. The obvious was they didn't stay in place, but the other was the stares some people gave me. Or the occasional smirk. Or even the confused look from people who never had to deal with that kind of issue.

Annoying people who couldn't mind their own business.

And so I stepped outside again, as though I was submerged into boiling water. It wasn't just the heat that was too much, but the humidity. Thirty degrees Celsius is doable in dry heat, but when the humidity adds an extra fifteen, and it felt like forty-five? Hell would be proud.

As I approached the building, black spots darkened the side of my vision. With my luck, I'd pass out before being able to step inside. Or worse, I'd make it in and look a mess when meeting this guest professor for the first time.

Way to make a first impression.

We'd spoken on the phone and corresponded by email for the last week, but meeting in-person was different. Hopefully, there was a washroom somewhere in there where I could at least clean up a bit beforehand. I checked my phone for the time, put it away, then pulled it back again when I realized I didn't even register what time it was. Ten minutes to spare; it was a good thing I was always anxious about being late and showed up everywhere at least thirty minutes in advance. Not that I'd go in that early, but it gave me time to mentally relax, make sure I looked presentable, and most important of all, go in without panting like I'd run a marathon.

I entered the old house-turned-offices, and my whole body thanked me for the blast of cool air. Even my mind seemed to stop heating my brain fluid almost instantly. I still had a few minutes to spare, but the office number was upstairs, and with no elevators, I'd need time to catch my breath once I was up there. There was no time for a wash-room check.

Grabbing the railing, I gripped it hard and began walking up the steps. My legs shook; I'd already walked more than usual in the past few minutes, and additional stairs weren't welcome. As I reached the top, I wiped at the sweat pooling along my upper lip, then did my best to push my hair back from my sticky forehead.

The office in question was closed, and no lights seemed to be coming from behind the door. Part of me wanted to cry while another wanted to scream profanities, but instead, I just stood there, deflated. Too tired to care anymore. Why wasn't he here? I'd bothered to make an appointment with the man, came all the way to his office only for him to have moved without letting me know, and then walked to the new location, and still...

I gritted my teeth, trying my best to calm down so I didn't burst into tears at how exhausted I was.

Another office door opened, and a young man poked his head out. "Oh, hello. Are you here to see Professor Frauley?"

"Yes," I said, still a bit breathless. "I had an appointment with him. My name is Jill."

He nodded, then stepped out. "The professor said you'd be coming around this time but that you might be a bit late." He rubbed the back of his head, ruffling his black hair. "I'm Patrice, a teacher's assistant. I was supposed to email you about the new location, but we're having issues with the internet in here, and phones don't get service either." His gaze traveled from my feet and back to my eyes. "I'm sorry you walked all the way there for nothing."

So it was obvious; I likely looked disheveled. I debated between telling him it was okay or that he should try the trek I just did, but instead, I took out my phone again. Low and behold, I had no service in this place, so I decided to forgive him.

I shrugged. "It's fine. Technology just doesn't work when we want it to, right?" I said with a smile.

"Yeah, sorry again." He motioned toward the professor's door. "He had to go out for a last-minute meeting but said I could use Professor Corriveau's office to start with the meeting since I'm the one who did most of the research about your questions—"

"If it's okay, I'd rather just wait for Professor Frauley since I also needed to talk to him about something more...personal." I fidgeted with my bag, unsure how much Patrice knew about why I was here.

"You mean about his connection to the man you're looking for?" When I nodded, he smiled. "I actually have the professor's notes about that as well, but as soon as he gets back, you can definitely ask him more questions about it."

My heart skipped a couple of beats. The professor had left notes about when he was a practicing psychologist and might have seen the serial killer as a patient. This would change all my plans about how I'd go about writing my article.

"In the meantime," Patrice's voice brought me back to the present, "I still have that research you needed if you're interested in looking at it over with me."

"That sounds good, thanks."

He waved his hand toward the office, and I stepped inside. The door closed behind with a loud click, and a tiny shiver ran down my spine. I guessed it was the drastic temperature change and pushed away my unease as I took a seat.

Patrice walked around the desk and sat in the leather chair. "So you wanted information about the last few recorded homicides and suicides in the city within the past few years, correct?"

"Yes."

Patrice opened one of the desk drawers and pulled out a thick folder. "I didn't know how many of the deaths was a few, so I grabbed the last twenty." He slid it toward me. "I included attempted murders as well."

"Thanks." My heart pounded in my chest at the thought of comparing these notes to the ones I had back at my apartment. Maybe I'd actually be able to make a connection. After putting the folder safely into my bag, I turned back to Patrice. "Have you been a TA for long?"

He shook his head. "No. Pretty new."

The phone on the desk rang, and I jumped at the sudden noise. It would definitely make sense to have a landline if the internet and Wi-Fi didn't connect well in this old building, but then, Patrice could've called me...

"I'll be right down," Patrice said before hanging up.

I wanted to point out he could've made a phone call,

but before I could say anything, he got to his feet. "Sorry, I need to run downstairs quickly. Professor Corriveau's been waiting for this delivery since yesterday, and it needs a signature. I don't want him to miss it." He grabbed a bag from the floor and dashed toward the door. "Mind staying here while I get it?"

"Sure..."

The door closed again, and I sat back, letting out a breath. Exhaustion settled within; the day was suddenly catching up to me. Right before my whole walking journey, I'd helped grade papers for a first-year psychology class. Most of which read more like novels than research writing. They'd learn, though, as everyone did.

After four years, I'd completed my bachelor's degree in journalism and had moved on to my master's. But with only eight months left before my final report was due, time suddenly seemed to be moving too fast. It would all come to an end soon enough.

Deciding I wasn't going to wait around any longer, I got to my feet and went to the door. I tried turning the doorknob but frowned when it didn't budge.

"What the..." I stared at it, noticing the keyhole as my heart hammered against my chest. The doorknob was installed the other way around. He'd locked me in from the outside.

My breath came faster as I backed away. No, it just had to be a mistake. It was likely one of those doorknobs that required a key both ways, and Patrice hadn't thought of it when he'd closed the door.

Still, I hated being locked inside an office, and soon, the walls were closing in. I needed a distraction. I pulled out my phone, scrolling on a few pages before remembering the internet didn't connect here, nor was there any service to call out. More and more, the room shrunk, and I paced. I clutched at my throat, desperate for more air, but none came.

"Calm down. Relax. Everything's fine," I mumbled as I stopped in front of one of the shelves.

Books stood along the wooden surfaces, filling it from top to bottom. Books were a good distraction, so I grabbed at a random one, but a plastic box that looked like six books slid out.

They were fake.

I pulled out more, but none of them were real. Even the pictures inside the frames were generic ones that came with when purchasing them. What was going on? Why was everything inside this office fake? And where was Patrice? How long did it take to sign for a package?

I couldn't breathe anymore; it was as though someone had wrapped a rope around my neck and was cutting off the oxygen. The heavy curtains over the window helped keep the heat out, but I needed sunlight—something to show me there was a real world beyond this artificial place.

My stomach churned when I opened them, revealing nails keeping the window shut tight. I spun, and the opened laptop caught my attention. Or, more accurately, the video playing on the screen. I approached the desk and leaned my trembling hands on the surface, staring at Patrice lying in a pool of blood somewhere. With the little light coming into the room, I guessed the basement, the cement floor looking frozen as his body convulsed.

Someone else came into view and crouched next to Patrice. The knife in the stranger's hand glistened crimson. I pressed my hands against my mouth as he pushed the blade against the young man's throat, then sliced through in one sure motion.

It wasn't the first time this person had done this. No hesitation. No trembling hands. Nothing.

He stood and turned toward the camera. I swallowed the bile at the back of my throat as he waved. He wore a black mask, the eyes darkened out, and a smile cut out into a slit. The serial killer I was tracking... It was him.

He stared at the ceiling, then vanished from view.

"Oh my God," I whispered, then stared up toward the door. He was coming for me.

I grabbed the chair I'd been sitting on only moments ago and placed it at an angle so it was wedged under the doorknob. At least it would give me a few seconds before he likely bashed his way inside. No. I wouldn't die today. It wasn't my time. I hadn't written my report yet.

Grabbing the second guest chair, I dragged it toward the window, then smashed it against the glass as hard as I could. It bounced back, leaving behind only a tiny crack. Why couldn't it be easy like in the movies?

I did it again, this time using all my strength as I pictured the killer reaching the top of the stairs. The glass shattered, and I jumped back as shards flew to the floor and outside. I gripped one of the curtains, wrenched until it ripped off a good amount, then tied it to the professor's leather chair. Being on the second floor, I needed a way to climb down; I just hoped this part worked a bit better than the glass smashing.

The doorknob jingled, and I almost threw up as my stomach clenched. I took hold of the curtain and tugged. The long chair angled itself horizontally, allowing me to climb down along the brick wall of the old house. Heat burned through my sandals, but I didn't care. I could barely feel it.

As soon as my feet hit the ground, I ran off toward the street, needing to be in view of the public as much as possible. Not because I'd be asking for help, but because if the killer came after me, he likely wouldn't do anything in broad daylight in front of everyone.

My chest heaved as I stared toward the house from across the street.

That was too close. But it also meant I was getting closer to figuring him out.

2

IMAGINATION

*S*uddenly, the heat didn't seem to matter as much as I took detour after detour before heading to my apartment. I wasn't about to take a chance he was following me.

As the sun slowly set behind the buildings, though, I finally headed home. I kicked off my sandals as soon as I stepped inside my apartment, then locked the door behind me. Three locks and a chain for good measure. I knew what break-ins could leave behind, and I didn't intend to be another dead body.

A separator gave off the illusion of having my own bedroom, but it was still a studio. I switched on the lights, illuminating the tiny kitchen; I was pretty lucky to have an island counter that gave me more space at least. Not that I enjoyed cooking much, and I barely had the time to bake even if I wanted to.

I sat on my sofa and placed the folder on my coffee table, staring at it as though it may explode. It was still a dangerous item to have in my possession. It was from

Professor Frauley and given to me by Patrice. And now he was dead.

Grabbing the remote next to me, I turned on the television and flipped through the channels. No cable or streaming services, but a few were free without a subscription. I stopped on the news, my heart hammering against my chest as I recognized the location where the reporter stood.

At first, I barely registered the words but focused instead on the text below the woman reporting on a grisly murder that took place on the University of Ottawa's campus. A man was found dead, stabbed to death with his throat slit, in the basement of a house-turned-office.

My stomach churned as I sat on the edge of the cushion, the words finally sinking in as they announced Patrice Talbot as the name of the deceased. He'd been a student at the University of Ottawa, currently working on his bachelor's in theater.

Theater? Bachelor?

He couldn't have been a teacher's assistant then. Why had he lied about that?

More news continued, and they announced the last person to have seen Patrice was none other than Professor Frauley, who was missing.

I bit my lower lip, trying to figure out what to do about the whole thing. I'd had an appointment with the professor, so the police would likely come speak with me. It was an easy enough lie to say I saw the paper posted on the main office's door, and because of the heat, I decided not to go. If they asked why I didn't call to let him know, I could just invent something about the fact that the professor obviously hadn't bothered letting me know about the change of location, so I didn't feel the need to call him and cancel either.

It always scared me a bit, just how fast I could come up with lies, but it was how I'd survived with a lot of my foster families. When used correctly, it was a perfect shield.

Leaving the television on, I stared at the folder in front of me. If the killer had been in the professor's office, had he been able to access my school profile? Did he torture him to get the information, or had Frauley given it willingly in the hopes of living?

Thankfully, I hadn't given my real address, and my mailing one was for a postal box near the university. I still had a pang of guilt for whoever did live at that fake address. Not that the killer would likely target them; it was random, but there were intervals between each victim, and after Patrice, he wouldn't kill for at least a month.

Checking Professor Frauley's notes, I found the name and phone number for the patient he'd seen, but the note next to it said he'd moved.

I pulled out my smartphone and tapped the screen for my image gallery instead by accident. It was such a habitual thing for me since I often took photos of notes, papers, and books for references when working on my report. The photo of the note posted to Professor Frauley's door caught my attention, and I stared at the phone number on it. I quickly scrolled through the few contacts I had, then compared the professor's number to the one on the paper.

It wasn't the same.

My breath came in quicker. Was it Patrice's number? Or had this been an elaborate plan by the killer to lure me somewhere secluded so he could get rid of everyone who'd been researching him. Was that why Patrice was dead? And wasn't it likely the same fate had befallen the professor? Because they'd dug into the current murders at my request?

"Well...shit," I muttered as I grabbed the remote and switched off the television now that it was talking about sports.

The apartment was plunged into silence, and I closed my eyes, trying to calm down, but knowing they'd probably gotten killed because of me didn't sit right at all. It was one thing to accept death and even have a morbid curiosity about it, but I didn't want to be responsible for other people. Not again.

I looked back down at the phone number and, on a whim, dialed it. It went to a generic voicemail, but something in my gut told me to leave a message. That this was for the killer.

"I'll be in the study room in the basement of the archives tomorrow evening if you want to meet there. I have questions I'd like to ask." I hung up, already going over what I'd tell the authorities if they'd ask me about why I'd left that message in case it did belong to one of the two murdered men. They'd definitely know a third person was there at some point... Could be any student, but I'd had an appointment planned, and telling them I just changed my mind about going because of the distance wouldn't remove me from the suspect list. If anything, they'd likely assume I lied, and I'd be put up higher on that list.

It was stupid to have left a message, but at this point, it was too late to take it back. There were a lot of things I'd done in my life I couldn't take back; I'd just add this one to the list.

I got to my feet and stretched, my back cracking in a few places as I did. It was definitely time for bed, if I could manage to sleep after everything. I appreciated being able to rest without the fear of someone sneaking into my bed at night. The first time it had happened, I was around thirteen years old. It wasn't anything too bad compared to what I went through later, but that first time was...a lot.

I closed the laptop with a snap and strode to the room separator. This tiny section of my studio held my bed, a small dresser, and a nightstand, all of them in the fake black wood that was more plastic than natural, but it fit my theme. Everything was dark in color, except for what I wore. But I wasn't picky about that on scorching days.

I rummaged around in my drawers trying to find the right pajamas for the weather, but then scoffed. Why was I bothering with clothes at all? I lived alone and could sleep naked in this heat if I wanted to. But then the thought of the killer entering my apartment slid into my mind, and my pulse shot straight down between my legs.

I clenched my jaw. "What's wrong with me?" I asked myself for the thousandth time. No number of psychologists had ever helped with what the world called *trauma*, but to me, it was my way to cope. My way to gain back the sexuality that belonged to me and me alone.

My fingers brushed against something hard, and I grabbed the old pill bottles I'd kept in case. Codeine. Just the thought of relief sent my heart fluttering in my chest. No pain. When I took these, it was as though I floated away into a dreamless sleep—one that wasn't plagued with nightmares or sex. But the more I took, the less they worked, and that was beyond annoying. It was the one thing that got me to stop...eventually. But not before that last time with Lee and his friends.

At the thought of my last sexual escapade, my pussy clenched, and I let out a shuddering breath. Sex with Lee was for discounts on the codeine, nothing else. He was objectively good looking, but I saw him for the scum he really was and just didn't care for him. And I knew for a fact he didn't like me, often calling me names, and belittling me. Not in the way I wanted it but really just to be mean.

Still, he fucked me rough like I enjoyed. Not quite hard enough, but better than I'd had so far in life. Ironically, I'd had more sexual relationships before I'd turned eighteen than as an adult, and part of me had always blamed my social worker's help. I'd suddenly had food on the table and never went hungry. And soon enough, I ate my stresses, my anxieties, as well as my joys and victories. Any excuse, really.

I stripped down until I was naked, then sat on the edge of my bed. Part of me didn't actually want to get off tonight; I still had the image of Patrice getting murdered seared into my memory. Yet again, the thought of the killer with the mask crawled into my mind and settled there. I pictured him unlocking my door with ease, using a hook of sorts to undo the chain as well. He'd walk inside, and despite his steel-toed boots, he wouldn't make a sound as he approached where I slept.

He'd stare at me, sleeping naked, the sheet barely covering any part of me… Goosebumps covered my skin, and I opened the drawer to my nightstand to grab the vibrating dildo. It wouldn't be the killer in the mask, but I could definitely use my imagination.

3

EXCHANGE

After leaving a voicemail for a potential serial killer, I decided it was time for me to put into motion my contingency plan to keep from becoming another murder victim. I headed toward the Rideau Center, hoping Martin worked today; I needed his help more than ever.

The cool air hit me like a ton of bricks, and I shivered as my sweaty skin turned icy. I rubbed my arms as I followed the crowd of people coming off a bus, keeping up with the pace of the busy city life.

Having grown up in a small town just on the other side of the river, it had taken some time to get used to the hustle and bustle of everyday life here. Luckily for me, I was used to stress.

As I approached the computer store, I spotted Martin inside, typing on one of those fancy tablets that would take months of savings to buy. After all, the only money I made was from my job as a teacher's assistant and the bursaries from my good grades.

"What's up?" Martin said with a grin as he finished

with something on the screen. When he looked at me with his baby blues, his smile vanished. "Whoa... you okay? You're pale as a ghost."

"Thanks. You look great, too," I said sarcastically. "I'm here about the laptop." Martin was a good friend, and a serial killer toying with me wasn't something I wanted to drag him into, but I'd run out of choices. "Were you able to finish with it?"

"Yeah, it's all done. Quite the complex software..." He arched an eyebrow at me as though waiting for an explanation, but when I pressed my lips together, he rolled his eyes. "It's like that again?"

"Look, you know what my final report is about," I whispered, leaning forward to make sure no one overheard us. "Can you blame me for being paranoid from time to time?"

"I really wish you weren't so obsessed with serial killers." He crouched and, when he straightened, put my laptop on the counter. "Your phone is connected to it as well, as you asked."

"Perfect."

He pushed the device aside and leaned his forearms against the white counter. The piercings on his face caught the overhead lights, making them almost glow. "Am I going to get into any type of trouble for this, Jill?"

"No..." When he gave me a look, I repeated the statement with more certainty, "No." The serial killer didn't need to know who created the program for me, only that it was the one way that would keep him from just instantly adding me to his victim list.

"You know if this comes back to me and the police ask questions..."

"It'll be okay." I forced a smile.

"Usual exchange as agreed, then?" He pushed his bleach blond hair from his face. "I actually have a break coming up in a few minutes."

My heart beat a bit faster as my cheeks warmed. It wasn't the first time I traded a blowjob for free help with computers, but any time we did anything intimate, it just made my crush on him grow deeper. Even though I knew he'd never go out with me officially since I wasn't the type of girl he'd date. I'd seen the ones he was with, and they were always fit and active—the opposite of me.

"I'll meet you at the usual spot then?"

"Yeah, I'll finish with the laptop. Wanted to double-check there isn't any kind of tracking on it." He bopped my nose playfully before turning his attention back to the device. "I'll see you in about ten minutes?" he asked, not looking back up at me.

I nodded but added, "Sure."

Our usual spot.

A washroom for the disabled on the same floor where he worked. So romantic. It was rarely ever used. A few people went inside to do drugs or even sleep, but that was mostly at night. During the day, it remained empty save for the occasional sexual acts between me and Martin whenever we were both horny or I needed a favor. When it was for an exchange, it was always a blowjob. The first few times, I'd felt so used and dirty afterward, but the more I did it, the less it bothered me. It wasn't like when my foster father had forced me to do the same thing. With Martin, it was different. It was consensual. It was my choice.

Down the long and empty hallway toward the washrooms, I couldn't help but wonder how I'd gotten to this point in my life. A blowjob in exchange for safety. A serial killer who knew I was looking into him. Watching a murder happen through video live. And yet, I barely felt any of it. Numb to the world despite my one drive: write and publish my report.

I supposed having been the only survivor of a home invasion when I was fifteen years old and watching as my foster parents were killed might have to do with my feelings about my whole situation. But I'd hoped since starting the program recommended by my social worker that the darkness lingering inside me would've vanished by now. Yet, at the age of twenty-seven, I still didn't mind the morbid side of death. On the contrary, I was fascinated by it.

The washroom was empty, as predicted, and I stepped inside. My pulse still didn't slow at the whole situation; it still seemed insane the killer had been there, waiting. How? And why had he killed Patrice? I closed the toilet seat and sat, running my fingers through my hair and gripping it. Sure, I didn't mind the subject of death, but having come so close to it only dawned on me then and there. He would've murdered me for sure, right? What else could he want?

At the thought of having my throat sliced open, or drowned, stabbed...depending on the card I chose, I shivered. If I was right about how he worked, he was using four cards, all Jacks, and always left behind a deck of cards at the scene with a missing Jack. Through research, I'd figured it out and confirmed my suspicions. It was why his method of killing varied so much; it was determined by the chosen card.

There was a small knock at the door, and I jumped. A small part of me hesitated. What if it was the killer? I scoffed at my imagination but still didn't unlock it as I approached.

"Occupied," I called out, not too loud.

"It's me," Martin hissed through his teeth. I opened the door, he stepped inside. "What the hell? Usually, the knock is enough."

"Oh, terribly sorry to inconvenience you," I said, crossing my arms. "I told you I'm a bit more paranoid than usual. What do you expect?"

"Some logic, maybe?" he said with a scoff. Still, he handed me the laptop.

"Thanks," I said in a shaky voice as I put the device into my messenger bag.

When I straightened, he gripped the back of my neck and pulled me close. "How much do you appreciate it?" he asked in a low voice.

My pulse quickened faster than the thoughts of murders and serial killers. Martin wanted me. Desired me. Not in public, but in private, at least.

I slowly got down on my knees, the tiles cold against my skin. They creaked beneath me, but I didn't care. None of it mattered except for pleasuring Martin. My feelings for him only seemed to grow when he looked at me that way... like I was the only woman in the world for him. Even if only in that moment.

Lifting his t-shirt, I took the time to run my hands along his narrow waist, his tight, flat belly hot to the touch. I undid his jeans, tugging on them until they slid down his long, muscular thighs. He wasn't wearing anything beneath, and my panties pooled in warmth at the sight of his growing arousal. He was already hard for me, and that just made the throbbing between my legs more intense.

I enjoyed being down on the floor this way while he towered over me. It made him seem more dominant, even if he wasn't really. I could picture him grabbing me by the hair and pushing his cock down my throat. But he never touched me or looked at me while I took him in my mouth. He just closed his eyes and groaned.

Flicking my tongue across the head of his bulging erection, he jerked, his eyes shutting as usual. This time, he caressed the side of my cheek, and that touch alone sent butterflies fluttering through my stomach.

I took him into my mouth, swirling my tongue around his rigid shaft. Moving my hands along the same rhythm, I slurped and suckled, picturing him fucking me from behind like he did sometimes. How he'd pounded into me hard and fast, hitting my sensitive spot at just the right angle. Then again, it wasn't difficult for me to reach climax; it actually didn't take much at all.

He let out a shuddering breath, and I knew he was close to orgasm. I took his erection down my throat, swallowing around it multiple times, doing my best to breathe through my nose despite gagging a few times. Tears ran down my cheeks as I imagined him holding me in place, hands tied behind my back, taking what was his. In my imagination, I enjoyed being roughed up. It was one of the ways I was always able to cum so fast.

Having his erect manhood down my throat hurt, but the pain only heightened my orgasm as an explosion of ecstasy ran down my body. I moaned against him, then played with his balls, rolling them between my fingers as I sucked harder against his member. He groaned low, and his hot seed spilled into my mouth, trickling down my throat.

Before I knew it, he helped me to my feet and gave me a quick kiss on the cheek. It was awkward, almost as though he'd forced himself to do it. Deflation hit me, but I forced a smile.

"Thanks again for the laptop."

He pulled his pants back up and buttoned up. "Yeah, no problem. And thanks for..." He cleared his throat, avoiding my gaze. "Thanks."

And without another word, he left me alone in the washroom.

4

WAITING

I finished writing the last of my notes, then jotted down the annotation. The book itself had seen better days; the paper thinned and had a musty smell to it. It was almost too dry to the touch, as though the material was flaking off. Or maybe it was just a lot of dust.

I closed it and began putting away some of my belongings before slowing my pace. No one had shown up yet, and part of me—an insane part—hoped the killer would. But maybe he didn't want to be seen, and having been here most of the evening, he hadn't had the chance to approach me. I glanced around; a few other students busied themselves with work at their own little cubicles. Leaving things unattended wasn't out of the ordinary when needing to use the washroom quickly, but I was always a bit nervous about it. Still, I needed to leave something behind so he'd know I was coming back.

I grabbed my messenger bag but left the rest. Drinks, empty wrappers, a few books, and some notes; a message to anyone seeing the desk that whoever was using it wasn't done with it yet. As I left the quiet room, chills ran along my skin at the sudden blast of air conditioner; apparently, someone wanted to pretend they lived in the Arctic in this particular corridor. That or the thing was busted.

The washroom was tiny, only two stalls. But with one on every floor, they didn't need to be much bigger. Not as though people spent hours in here usually. I picked the one against the wall and sat on the toilet, trying not to think of the germs I could be getting. Hovering wasn't an option; I'd likely lose my balance and fall face-first on the floor. Not a position I wanted paramedics to find me in. And if I covered the seat with toilet paper, it would likely stick to my sweaty thighs more than anything.

The door to the washroom opened, and I stiffened. Heavy boots stepped forward, the sound of the metal on the sides clicking against the zippers. My heart hammered in my chest as I held my breath, waiting for the stall door to suddenly break down and have a maniac brandishing a knife at me.

Instead, the door opened again, and someone else walked in.

"So are we going to Dominion's tonight or not?" a woman asked in a hushed tone.

There was a scoff. "Of course. Where else can we get wasted at those prices?"

My shoulders relaxed, and I pressed my hand against my mouth to keep from snickering out loud. Here I was, assuming a serial killer had actually taken the bait and came to find me in the women's washroom, of all places. There were people around, and the man had eluded being found out for years; he wasn't stupid enough to show up here and murder someone without having done some research first.

I waited a bit, but when both women didn't seem to be leaving anytime soon, I flushed and left the stall. I glanced at the one next to mine and noticed the clogged toilet; that's why they'd been waiting for me to finish.

The one with the steel-toed boots gave me a quick nod before sliding in after me, while the other woman with the short dress crossed her arms and waited by the wall.

The air conditioning didn't work as well inside this area, and sweat had formed along my upper lip. I quickly wiped it away before turning on the tap and washing my hands. The cool water was nice for a second before it went warm.

The woman waiting for her turn rubbed the back of her neck and let out a sigh. "Are you sure we should go? I mean, we have to go by that shady area..."

"That's why it's cheap," the other one chimed from inside the stall. "Come on, it'll be fun."

I finished washing my hands, then grabbed some paper towels to dry them; although, in this humidity, I wasn't sure it was possible. I stared at the woman, unsure if I wanted to say anything. Part of me wanted to warn her about what to expect at Dominion's since she looked a bit... innocent, was the only word that came to mind.

But it wasn't my place, so I gave the girl a smile and then left. Again, the arctic air blasted me in the face, instantly making my sweat turn cold against my skin. I rubbed my arms a few times, trying to dry off, but I just shivered and picked up the pace.

Back in the quiet study area, I approached my desk, pulse throbbing in my ears as my gaze swept along the surface.

Nothing.

I let out a breath and grinned; of course there wouldn't be anything. I'd hoped there would be. Maybe a note or something to show he'd been here, looking for me. But that was stupid. And a dangerous hope to have, anyway. With a small shake of my head, I grabbed the rest of my stuff and headed out into the cold recycled air, then outside into the scorching heat. This kind of sudden change in temperatures couldn't be healthy, but with the way I was heading, there were deadlier things that would end up killing me.

As my footsteps echoed against the hot sidewalk, my mind wandered off to where it always went whenever someone mentioned the name Dominion's. In my first years of university, I'd gone to the club often, always looking for someone who might show interest in me. High school had been lonely since I'd shut myself away, and by the time I found any kind of self-confidence, I was too awkward for normal human interaction. Still, I'd made some friends—including Martin—but I'd found something else too. A drug dealer by the nickname Lee. He'd given me a free sample of opioids, and soon enough, all the pain I'd felt in my life had vanished away with just half of a small pill.

And despite knowing how the drug worked—or didn't—I was hooked. I'd given myself excuse after excuse to continue taking some. It was rare at first. Always half, even if it didn't work as well after a while. Then I had to start paying for the full dose. It wasn't cheap, and I didn't have the disposable income. But Lee was generous. He accepted a lower amount of cash as long as I gave him blowjobs too. A few times, I had no money at all and desperately needed another dose faster than expected, and for that, he was as generous as ever. All I needed to do was perform the same on his friends.

That night I was passed around was the last time I went to the nightclub. Not because of the shame but because one of those new friends I'd made, Ginette, over-dosed. Someone else died. Next to me. Because of me. I'd gotten her hooked just talking about the relief I'd felt when taking it. It was all my fault. Again. Death followed me everywhere as though I owed it my life.

It was that next morning I admitted to my social worker I had a problem. With her help, I was able to see a doctor and, from there, a psychiatrist who prescribed me small doses to eventually wean me off completely. I never went to the psychologist, though; bad experiences with them in the past. Didn't trust them after I saw one at thirteen, and he didn't believe what I told him.

I tightened my grip on the messenger bag as I approached Waller Street; if I turned down that road, it would bring me to Dominion's. To that wonderful high that took away all my anguish.

But I turned around and took the next street. Toward home instead. If I fell into drugs again, I wouldn't be able to write my report. Nothing was more important. Except maybe meeting the man I was writing it about.

5

SAFE SPACE

"Great. Another power outage," I muttered as I unlocked the door to the apartment complex where I lived.

It was so warm inside; I was sure everyone in the building had turned off their ACs and switched on their ovens instead. It was likely because it was an old place, so the electrical wires didn't work as well anymore. Still, on a hot night like this, not having electricity really sucked.

I walked up the stairs to the second floor, then into the hallway lit only by the emergency lights. It gave the place an eerie feel, as though I wasn't supposed to be here because it was closed or something. Sweat trickled down my back as I unlocked my door and stepped inside. If it was possible, it was even stuffier in my studio apartment. I locked the door behind me, sliding the chain in its place as I kicked off my sandals. The outside noise muffled through the windows and curtains; I'd closed them before leaving to keep the place as cool as possible, but it obviously hadn't done much. How long had the power been out?

With a sigh, I pulled out my smartphone and tapped

the screen until the little flashlight button turned orange. It would be good enough while I searched for candles, but I didn't want to drain my battery for too long. This was my only alarm clock for mornings.

As I approached the island counter, my pulse sped as I noticed a folded piece of paper standing on the surface. With my light pointed at it, it seemed like the most threatening thing in the world. Goosebumps crawled along my arms and legs, and I held my breath as I picked it up.

I got your message.

I trembled as the air around me turned cold.

My heartbeat pulsed in my ears. The city sounds from outside vanished.

Everything behind me was a threat, but I didn't dare turn around.

He was inside my apartment. Or had been.

Slowly, I put the paper back onto the counter and took in a shuddering breath. My eyes burned with unshed tears, instincts of fight or flight urging me to move. To do something.

I spun, swinging my arm out, but hit empty space. No one waiting behind me. The separator that was once something for privacy seemed to be hiding death. The bathroom, a place to hide. Even the closet by the door wasn't safe.

I swallowed hard and winced as my throat tightened. What was I supposed to do? I wouldn't call the police, but staying was beyond stupid.

So was leaving a message for the killer in the first place.

I stepped as lightly as I could back toward the entrance, slipping on my flip-flops; there wasn't any time for anything that required belts and buckles. The tiniest sound sent my adrenaline spiking. Despite my shaky hands, I managed to slide the chain lock off without any sounds. A shadow moved in the corner of my vision, and I wrenched the door open, grabbing my messenger bag before bolting out. It might have been nothing, but I hadn't thought of checking behind the island counter. Had he been crouched there, waiting?

Staring at the door, I debated what to do. Grabbing my baseball bat and searching the place came to mind, but in the dark, it was reckless. What if he wasn't even in there anymore?

Then how was the second lock bolted?

The only way he could've locked my door without a key would've been to lock the doorknob from the inside and just shut the door. I tried recalling whether I'd heard one click when I used my key, but my memory was blank. They just merged with every other time I'd unlocked both and walked inside.

Even if he'd left, the fact he'd been inside sent more shivers down my spine. He'd invaded my personal safe space, and going back seemed impossible. As though it wasn't even my place anymore. I glanced at my phone and switched off the flashlight, not wanting to waste more battery. Maybe Martin would let me crash at his place tonight?

I sent him a quick text—nothing too specific—then strode off downstairs toward the front doors to the building. As I rounded the corner, I spotted a figure near the entrance. For a second, I froze, then nearly dove back, hitting myself against the wall and scratching the side of my leg. I hissed through my teeth as I stared at the cut, already a line of red appearing. The decorative strip was cracked in a few places, and one piece jutted out at just the right angle to slice me.

My heart hammered as I peeked around the corner, swallowing against the tightness in my throat. The man stood with his back turned to me, black sweater with the hood pulled up. Who dressed that way in this weather? Was that him? Waiting for me?

I staggered back, glancing at my phone again, but no word from Martin.

"Shit... shit... shit," I muttered as I took off for the other exit.

I rarely used the side one since I didn't have a vehicle, but for this one time, I'd make an exception. Just as I stepped outside, my phone dinged, and I stopped in my tracks.

Martin: Sorry. Roommates have an agreement about no guests over.

"Fucking..." I slipped the phone back into my bag but took it out again, deciding I'd let Martin know how *great* of a friend he was being. He hadn't even asked what was wrong. Or asked if everything was okay to begin with. All he wanted from me was sex and blowjobs without anyone else knowing about it. He wasn't my friend at all.

That reality sunk in harder than it should have, and I let out a small sob. Pressing my lips together, I blinked several times, looking up at the sky to stop from crying. It wouldn't help. My shoulders slumped as I slipped the device into the bag again.

Where was I supposed to go? I didn't have many options. Call my social worker. Go to a shelter for the night. None of those sounded particularly good. But the thought of going back into my apartment when I didn't know where the killer was didn't sit well with me either.

A hand covered my mouth from behind. I screamed against the warm leather, squirming as my back pressed into a hard chest.

This was it.

His palm pressed against my nose, forcing me to

breathe through my mouth. The smell made my stomach churn. A sharp prick pinched into my neck, and my eyes widened as a needle punctured my skin. What felt like hot lead pushed into me, and no matter how hard I struggled, it only made the pain worsen. The world around me spun, and I closed my eyes to stop it. Even in darkness, I plunged deeper into the void, steadied only by the man who came to take my life.

6

TRUST

A pounding headache throbbed against my temples. I squeezed my eyelids against the light seeping through. Had I overslept? What time was my alarm supposed to go off again? My mind blanked on when I set it last night before bed. Had the batteries run out? I recalled the power outage and groaned.

The note on my countertop flashed through my mind. I swallowed hard, the dull pain in my neck reminding me of what happened. My pulse quickened, and I sat up. Everything spun, and I pushed my hands against my face. A chain rattled, and I peeked from behind my fingers to the side.

Handcuffed to a chain.

Chained to a wall.

I let out a shaky breath as I pushed through the nausea. This had to be a nightmare. Yet as I stared down, the cot I'd been lying on was definitely not my bed. Before I wrapped my mind around the situation, the door opened, and a masked man walked in. I pressed my back against the wall, doing my best not to show fear. It had been one thing to see this man from behind the safety of some doors or through a video camera. Even looking through old photos of crime scenes he'd left behind. With him standing there, looming over me with the threat of the violence he could inflict, I had trouble breathing.

He grabbed a chair that stood in the corner of the room and dragged it in front of me. I stared around, but apart from the cot and chair, the room was empty. Without a word, he sat, and despite not being able to see his eyes, he was definitely staring at me. He pulled out a piece of paper, unfolded it, and held it up for me to see.

"I found an interesting message in your bag," he said in a low hum, the mask muffling his voice, but it was deep. The way I remembered it.

If you kill me, all my research gets sent to the police automatically. Please talk to me first.

My shoulders relaxed a little. Good. He'd gotten my note before he decided to do something drastic. Like murder me.

"I don't usually take orders, but you wrote down *please*, so I indulged..." He leaned forward a bit. "Don't make me regret it."

I opened my mouth to speak, but the dryness threatened to choke me. After a few seconds of silence, he put the paper back into his jacket pocket, the black material catching the light hanging overhead for a split second.

"I have... a proposition," I muttered, my voice wavering. How many times had I recited my speech in my mind? Out loud in the shower? "I'm doing a final report for my master's, and I want to interview you about your life and what you do."

He cocked his head, and a shiver ran down my spine as he seemed to take me in for the first time. "And why would I agree to that?"

"Because you'd be able to talk to someone about the people you've killed and will kill." I smiled. "I can't imagine there's a lot of people you can confide in—"

"Except for my victims. They'll take my secrets to the grave," he cut in, amusement lacing his every word.

I blinked a few times, wrapping my mind around his meaning. "I have a lot of information about you. Information that could easily lead the police to finding out your identity. What I'm asking..." I slowly sat up, allowing my bare feet to touch the cold cement floor as I straightened. "If you agree to be interviewed by me, I'll delete everything I have when I'm done."

"And if I say no and kill you right now?" He pulled out a knife, the blade contrasting against the all-black clothes he wore.

I stiffened. It was at least six inches, and the pain would be beyond horrible. Yet, at the same time, I knew how he killed, and it wouldn't necessarily be with this particular weapon.

Don't count on it. He just killed Patrice yesterday. You've thrown off his pattern.

"Every day, at nine o'clock in the evening, I input a PIN into software on my laptop or phone." I reached to the side, then realized my bag was missing, and so was my phone. I pushed my worry aside and continued, "If I don't input the code, everything I know about you is sent to the police's email address."

He fished into his pockets again and pulled out my phone. "And what makes you think I can't torture it out of you?"

"I'd give you the wrong one. You'd put that in, and then you'd have one last chance before it's sent out as a safeguard against that very thing." I shrugged, trying to act as though I wasn't terrified out of my mind. "I could give you a second PIN under torture, but if it's the wrong one..."

He chuckled as he handed me the device. "Clever."

I took it and arched an eyebrow. "Aren't you scared I'll call for help?"

"No." He twirled the blade in his hand. "Just as I wasn't worried you'd call the police when you found my note inside your apartment."

He was clever, too. But it didn't surprise me, considering how long he'd been a serial killer. As far as I knew, it had been at least twelve years.

"You weren't the man in the hoodie at the front of my building, were you?" I said, not really asking the question as I realized I'd walked right into his trap.

He shook his head. "In this economy, most people will do anything for a hundred dollars. Including wearing a hooded sweatshirt and standing outside a door for an hour. A desperate student might even play the role of a teacher's assistant to keep you inside an office..."

Oh, he was good.

"If you don't want to do the interview, I won't force you either. That wouldn't be ethical for my report—"

"As opposed to blackmailing me?"

"I'm not doing that. It's only in place if you torture or kill me." I adjusted the strap of my dress as it loosened, and I could've sworn his gaze followed the movement. Probably my imagination. "If you say no, then you give me a few days to disappear, and I promise I'll delete everything I have on you."

He laughed. A real laugh. No menace. My heart beat just a bit faster at the sound.

"And why should I trust you to do that?"

"Because trust is all we have. I trust you not to kill me, and you trust I won't send any of the information I have about you to anyone." I clutched the side of the cot. "You'll even be able to read my report before I send it out to my professor if you want to. Nothing will give out anything that can be traced back to you specifically."

Silence hung heavy between us for what seemed like forever. No sound came from anywhere but from the floor and walls, I guessed we were in a basement. Depending on how far from the city we were... I could be anywhere.

"Tell you what... I'll think about it."

It wasn't a 'no,' and I'd take it as a win. I couldn't help but beam as I clapped my hands together in excitement, the handcuffs clinking as I did. Glancing to the side, I stared at the loose chain next to me.

I lifted it up and grabbed another section with my other hand. "Isn't it a bad idea to have this much give in this chain? It could be used to wrap around your neck and choke you."

He leaned forward even more and dragged the chair until one of his knees pushed between my legs. "I dare you."

I couldn't breathe, but it wasn't just fear anymore. Something in his tone pushed me to act, and in one quick motion, I wrapped the metal links around him just as he pressed the knife against my throat. It was cool against my skin.

For a few seconds, no one moved or spoke. This close, the scent of wood and musk filled my nostrils.

"Are you always this obedient?" he asked; I could almost hear the smile.

I grinned, relieved he didn't decide to kill me. Instead, he seemed to find me amusing. "Only when it's malicious compliance." I let go of one end of the chain and slowly pulled away from him.

He chuckled as he lowered the knife. I waited for him

to unlock my cuffs, but when he didn't move, I lifted my arm. "I do have classes I need to be at before you make up your mind about the interview. If you don't mind..."

"And why would I let you leave?" he asked as though my request was absurd. "No. You can stay right here while I decide."

"I'm not inputting the PIN until you let me go, and when the cops find you—"

He stood and grabbed a fistful of my hair, yanking back as I gasped. "How do you know I'm not tired of this and want it to all end? Death by cop is easy. Quick." He traced the leather gloves along my cheek. "And I'd have twenty-four hours before that little timer of yours ran out. Do you know how much pain I could inflict in that time? How much I can bend you until you break? Don't mistake my curiosity for weakness, *darling girl*, or it's the last mistake you'll ever make."

I nodded despite the added strain it put against my scalp, and he let me go. Tears burned my eyes, but I ignored them as I massaged my head, wincing at the pain. "I have classes where they take attendance. If I don't show up, they'll let my social worker know, and she'll have my ass."

He strode to the door and vanished for a few seconds before returning with a syringe. "If you insist on leaving, then you're doing so the same way you came here."

"Can't I just close my eyes?" I asked, almost in a whine. I really hated needles.

"We've already established you're smart. I wouldn't put it past you to already have figured out where inside this place we are."

"Basement," I blurted out. I couldn't help it; his compliment about my intelligence made me tingle everywhere. "So does that mean you'll never invite me over to do the interview here?"

He approached, and I eyed the syringe as though it was worse than the knife.

"We haven't established whether I've agreed to that offer yet."

"Okay...but could you not stab me in the neck with it this time? That really hurt..."

He sat next to me on the cot, and I hoped he couldn't feel the heat coming off my body like I could his. "It has to go into the muscle," he said quietly as he took out a small packet from his pocket.

How many things does this man have in his pockets?

He ripped it open, then motioned at my upper thigh. "That's where it'll hurt the least. That or just below your shoulder." He traced a gloved finger on my back, just above my shoulder blade, and I couldn't help the tiny goosebumps spreading across my arms.

I swallowed against the dryness in my mouth. "Shoulder is fine," I muttered. "What is that, anyway?"

"A sedative. Midazolam."

He rubbed the pad on my skin, and I shivered at the sudden cold. Without another word, he pushed the needle in. I hissed through my teeth as the pressure grew. Instinctively, I leaned forward, trying to get away from the shot, but he grasped my arm, keeping me in place. His arm pressed against my chest, and I leaned into it, closing my eyes. The hot lead pushed into me again, and I clenched my jaw to keep from screaming.

Doziness hit me, and my head leaned against the sleeve of his leather jacket. For a second, I pictured him smiling, and something deep down inside felt like everything would be okay.

7

FOLLOWING

I had woken up on my couch. It was so surreal to be in my apartment after everything that happened. A quick shower woke me up, but I emailed my social worker saying I wasn't feeling well and wouldn't attend my classes. Thankfully, there were only two, and both professors posted the notes online.

A knock at the door churned my stomach, and I just stared at it for a few seconds before walking to it. Had he already made up his mind? Would he just kill me? If it was him, and he agreed, I'd give him a piece of my mind about injecting me for nothing.

How did he carry me in here?

Before I guessed at scenarios, Nina's face came into view from my peephole, and I sighed. I loved the woman, but Nina had a habit of showing up when I really just wanted to be alone.

Still, I owed my life to this woman. More than once. So I opened the door.

"You don't look sick," Nina said, walking in past me.

"Good morning to you, too."

Nina sat at the island counter and arched an eyebrow. "It's the afternoon."

"Then good afternoon," I said, closing the door and locking it. "Please, come in."

Nina ignored the sarcastic comment and dug into her purse. "So why are you missing classes today? That's not like you. Did something happen last night?"

If I could remember my mother, I hoped she'd been similar to Nina—no-nonsense but caring.

"Yeah, the power was out, so I had no air conditioning. Tossed and turned all night, couldn't sleep. Was too hot," I wanted to add I'd been drugged—twice—and kidnapped but thought it best to keep that to myself. Didn't want to worry my social worker and all.

Nina frowned. "Second time this summer this building had a power outage." She motioned toward the fridge. "Well, since I'm here, do you need any groceries? I can drive you if you want."

For a second, I was about to refuse but thought better of it; getting a ride in this heat would save me so much strain. Plus, I'd be able to buy a bit more than when I took the bus. "That would be great, thanks."

As we stepped into the summer heat, I squinted into the sunlight beaming down. I put away my keys, scoffing at the thought of locking my doors; it apparently didn't keep *some* people out.

Nina's car was still cool from the AC, and I couldn't help but be thankful for the quick departure. If we'd waited even a few minutes more, the inside would cook us alive. It often reminded me of the RV I lived in with my first foster parents. None of that fancy cooling system since it was too expensive, so the small space was always hot in the summer.

"So, how are things going with your report?" Nina

asked as she took a turn toward a busy street. Afternoon rush for lunch breaks were almost as bad as rush hour in the morning and evening. Great. It meant small talk.

"I've got regular semester starting up in a week, and I have until the end of April to submit it..." I didn't want to add a vital part of writing it required the interview. "I'm just waiting to hear back on whether I can get access to some potential information that could help."

"I wish you didn't write about such a morbid thing," Nina said, and just as I opened my mouth to argue, Nina raised her hand. "I know, I know. You've already explained why, and I get it to an extent. It's a way to deal with your trauma. I just worry about you sometimes."

So do I.

I shrugged. "It has less to do with my past as it does with the journalism degree I have. Most of my electives were in forensic psychology, and I took a lot of criminology courses to add to that type of knowledge. Serial killers as the main subject for my final report isn't out of the ordinary." I waved my hand in front of my face, trying to cool off a bit more; even the air conditioning was having trouble combating this heat.

"Yes, but considering what you went through when you were fifteen, I'd hoped—"

"I know you have my best interest at heart, and while I appreciate it, I already submitted my report subject to my professor months ago. He accepted it, so changing it isn't even possible if I wanted to." I turned to look at Nina. "Which I don't."

Nina nodded. "Alright, I get it. I know you hate being nagged. I'll drop it. Just make sure you take care of your mental health while you do all that research, okay?"

"I will."

Nina pulled the car into the parking lot of the giant grocery store, and with a grimace, I exited back into the heat. Thankfully, it was a short walk into the frigid air—much shorter than if I'd taken the bus—and soon enough, the summer dress I wore didn't keep me warm enough in the refrigerated aisles.

Nina pointed out a few things as we shopped, picking up a few personal things of her own along the way. A few times, I could've sworn someone was watching me, but I brushed it aside. The store was packed with people, and someone was bound to look in my direction at some point. It was ridiculous to be this paranoid.

"Do you want to finish up and meet me past the cash registers?" Nina asked, and I nodded, tightening my hand on the cart.

I lingered in front of the ice cream, looking back and forth between mint chocolate chip and chocolate cherry, unsure which I wanted more. Back a few years ago, I would've indulged in both, but I was learning to deal with my impulse control and not eating my stress. Especially when it contained that much sugar. With a sigh, I mentally calculated how much everything else would cost and decided on neither. I didn't need them and could save the money for more groceries in the next few weeks instead. People walked by, and as I grabbed the last few items I needed, I slowed my steps.

The scent of wood and musk seemed to surround me for a second.

I spun, staring around as though I'd suddenly see the masked serial killer standing at the end of the aisle. Waiting to run at me and take my life. I almost snorted at the image in my mind; the man was smart, and this was the last place he'd show himself.

Although, his taunting voice resonated in my mind about death by cop. I swallowed hard and pushed on, making my way to the registers.

The ride back was much quicker, but Nina still managed more small talk. "Any plans this weekend?"

My gaze darted to the side, sure for a second a figure clad in black stood on the sidewalk as they drove by. I glanced back, but no one was there, and I let out a small laugh.

Was I losing my mind?

"What's so funny?" Nina asked.

"Nothing. Was just thinking about something." I shook my head as I straightened in my seat. "And no plans."

"Are you still seeing Martin from time to time?" The question was innocent enough, but I knew better; Nina never liked the type of relationship I had with the guy. And at this point, I had to agree with her. Still, I'd never admit to that.

"Saw him yesterday. Fixed my laptop for me. Life saver, really, or I might have lost all my notes." When Nina arched an eyebrow and waited expectantly, I scoffed. "I'm not seeing him again *that* way any time soon."

"Oh? Did something happen?" Nina pulled up in the parking spot reserved for visitors.

Before Nina could ask more questions, I jumped out the car and headed for the trunk. It popped open, and I grabbed the four bags, happy with my haul. Deciding it would be rude to just leave, I went to the driver's side and smiled.

"Nothing happened. I'm just realizing it might not be a healthy relationship. A bit too one-sided." I lifted the bags. "Thanks again for the ride. I really appreciate it. Especially in this weather."

Nina grinned. "Take care of yourself, and no more missing classes."

"Noted. I've got the weekend to recuperate, so I'll be fine for Monday... unless we get another power outage." I wasn't lying; without even so much as a fan, it was impossible to sleep without electricity. Unless drugged.

8

CONDITION

$\mathcal{M}$y studio apartment was nice and cool this time as I stepped inside. I locked the door behind me, chain and all, then put the bags down so I could take my sandals off.

Footsteps approached, and I straightened, heart pounding. The killer walked out of my bathroom, the black mask as menacing as ever.

"Jesus Christ," I shouted, grabbing the baseball bat by my door and holding it up. My mind caught up with everything, and I slowly lowered the weapon. "Don't fucking do that!"

"Language, young lady," he said in a dark tone.

My eyebrows shot up; he was serious. I laughed, shaking my head. "Seriously? Swearing is where you draw the line? Not at killing?"

"We all need our morals and values," he said with a shrug. He took a seat on the armchair and waited in silence.

I felt almost silly still holding my weapon, but considering who I was dealing with, I wasn't sure he wouldn't decide to lunge and attack. "Are you here to talk or murder?"

"Depends." He spoke so matter of fact; it was as though he'd answered what his plans were for the weekend.

I put the bat back in its place and finished unlacing my sandals before grabbing the bags. The island counter was suddenly the perfect barrier between me and death. "I just need to put these away so they don't spoil..." I wasn't sure if I was asking permission or just nervous about having a serial killer in my home—again—but I didn't wait for his reply.

The fridge looked a bit fuller, but when I opened the freezer, my pulse throbbed in my ears. Two pints of mint chocolate ice cream and chocolate cherry ice cream stood at the forefront. Both his hands leaned on either side of my body, and I spun, eyes widening as he stood in front of me.

How had he approached without a sound?

"You didn't pick a specific one, so I got both," he said almost in an annoyed tone. As though frustrated at not being able to guess which I would've chosen.

I swallowed against the lump in my throat, unsure what to feel in the whirlwind of emotions shaking me. So, he had been watching me at the store; it hadn't been my imagination or paranoia at all. But why had he taken the time to grab both the ice cream flavors I'd been looking at and buy them for me?

"Thank you..." I wasn't sure what else to say, and despite the AC in my place and the opened freezer at my neck, I was extremely warm.

He took the bread from my hand and slipped it past my head to put it into its place. Without another word, he walked away and sat on the armchair again. I finished putting everything away as fast as my trembling hands allowed. Why did he have to be so unpredictable? It drove me crazy.

When I was done, I took a seat on the sofa, regretting my choice of placement. The closest one to the armchair. "I'm guessing you're here to discuss my proposal?" I asked in a small voice. It was so unlike me to waver. As though he had some sort of power I couldn't fight against.

"I'd like to set a condition before I agree to this interview. As well as some clarification." He leaned back in the chair as though he was the most comfortable he'd ever been.

I, on the other hand, clenched the material of my dress into my fists, bunching it. "Let's start with clarifications, then?"

"Would this be a one-time interview, or does it span over several days?" He drummed his gloved fingers against the armrest. "Or are you expecting to follow me everywhere and also watch me... work?"

I gawked at him. Would he actually let me do that? I'd be a witness, something he never allowed as far as I knew. "Is that...a possibility? The second option, I mean..."

"Yes, but this is where my conditions come in," he said with amusement. "I'll ask something of you after every time you interview me."

"Something?" I repeated, arching an eyebrow. Did he want me to kill someone?

"For example, I might ask you a question about yourself. And I'll want the truth."

I thought on that for a few seconds. "The methodology for the interview is supposed to be done in an unbiased way. Getting to know the interviewee could skew——"

"That's my condition," he said with a shrug.

I thought of a few more arguments but had the feeling when this man made up his mind about something, there was no changing it. "Okay. But when I ask you questions, I want the truth, too."

"Agreed."

"Could you give me another example of doing something? I mean, I don't want to aid you in killing anyone if that's—"

"I'll never ask you to hurt someone or take their life." He leaned forward, and I stiffened to stop myself from backing away. "What I may ask you is to act as bait to lure someone out of somewhere."

I didn't care for that at all, but refusing might end up with him refusing the interview. And if he said no, I wasn't sure he'd give me the chance to disappear like I planned. Not to mention, it was a bit of a bluff since I didn't really want to start over someplace else. "I agree. Any other conditions?"

"No." He put out his hand, and I took it, shaking on their agreement. His palm was warm through the leather, and I let out a small breath, relieved he wouldn't kill me. Not this day, anyway.

He chuckled. "I'm surprised you didn't name any conditions yourself."

"Interviews are supposed to happen naturally. Putting conditions on my end would be detrimental to my data. The only thing I need to do on my end is input my PIN every evening." I scratched at my leg and winced when my fingernails caught the cut from the night before. I hissed through my teeth and twisted in my seat to look at the wound. There hadn't been time to disinfect it, and with the way this building was maintained—or rather, wasn't—I wouldn't be surprised if the cut got infected if I didn't do something about it soon.

I got to my feet and walked past him. "Excuse me a minute."

Inside the bathroom, I took out the rubbing alcohol and band-aids and set them on the tiny amount of counter I had next to the sink. The room was small, but it was enough for what I needed, and I wouldn't complain. Although doing acrobatics to try reaching my leg wasn't too fun.

He stepped into the doorframe, and I froze, staring up at him while sitting on the toilet seat. I hadn't closed the door; it always made me too claustrophobic, and I hadn't even thought of the fact I had someone in my home. He crouched, grabbing the makeup removal pad with alcohol I'd been trying to use on the wound. It reminded me of how he'd sat next to me when he'd drugged me the second time. It had been a lot gentler than the first. I rubbed my neck at the spot, recalling all too well the pain of being stabbed with a needle.

"Does the PIN change every day?" he asked so nonchalantly I didn't realize what he was really asking at first.

"It does. I get a random code sent by email I have to decipher each time."

"That's quite the software engineering skillset you have. And deciphering codes? You're interesting..." He opened the band-aid and put it against the cut, rubbing it with his thumb a few times.

I got to my feet, and at this angle, when he looked up at me, butterflies fluttered in my stomach. His eyes weren't ever visible, but I could sense his stare each time. Like in the grocery store. "Did...you want to start the interview now?" I asked in a quiet tone.

He straightened, towering over my five foot six; he was likely around six-four. Even with the jacket, his muscular arms bulged beneath the material. No wonder he could easily kill people; even with my bat, I likely didn't stand a chance.

"You seem nervous," he said, and I could hear the smirk.

"I don't like being..." I didn't want to tell him my fears. He could easily use them against me if he wanted to. "I'd like to step out of the bathroom and go back into the main room if you don't mind?"

He looked around, the black mask with the smile catching the light a few times. "You don't like being what?"

I was about to lie but remembered I agreed to his condition. Telling the truth was part of that. "Is this your favor for the day?"

He laughed and shook his head before stepping aside. "No. I have something else in mind."

A shiver shot down my spine with the way he said that.

9

FIRST

I took out my notebook. Loose pages stuck out at odd angles, and the front cover was cracked in a few places. Still, it was the most important object in my life, and it meant everything to me. I opened it to a blank lined page and readied my pen.

"I'll be referring to you as the subject when I'm writing notes, so nothing ever connects back to you, but do you have anything you want me to call you when we're talking?" I asked, sitting on the edge of the sofa. My heart hammered. This was finally happening. I couldn't tell if I was more excited or afraid, but in that moment, it didn't matter.

"I'll get back to you on that."

I nodded and jotted down the date and time. "What is your earliest memory?"

"So you can make sense of why I'm the way I am?" He cocked his head. "I hate to break it to you, but I had loving parents. Good childhood. Earliest memory is the first day of kindergarten. The teacher was kind, and I made some friends." He leaned forward, elbows against his knees, as those black eyeholes stared at me. "Not every serial killer has a traumatic backstory."

"I know. It depends on individuals. Nature versus nurture and all." I shrugged as I jotted down more notes. "I'm also not a psychologist or psychiatrist, though——"

"But you have knowledge of the subject."

He knew what my courses had been in, which meant he'd likely looked at my student profile. There wasn't any use in trying to hide it. "Yes."

"People are fascinating that way, aren't they? Put two in the same kind of environment, and they turn out vastly different."

"What about your adolescence?"

"Ah," he raised a finger, "that would be a subject for the next interview."

I nodded, making a note adolescence seemed to be a more difficult subject to talk about. "Did you have any siblings?"

"Only child."

After speaking some more, his answers got shorter and shorter, and I decided a break was in order. I closed my notebook and stretched the elastic to keep the cover closed. For a first interview, I was happy with the results. "Thank you. That was very helpful."

He reached into his jacket, and I scooted back with a small gasp as he pulled out a photo. "Now, now. I wouldn't kill you after just the one interview."

His gaze searched me as though trying to see if I'd caught his underlying meaning. "What a relief." I didn't bother hiding the sarcasm in my tone. He was all about subtle little jabs, and I wasn't above dishing it back.

He handed me the picture. "You recall how I gave the example of being bait?"

"Seriously? You're starting with a huge favor?" I took

the photo and stared at the profile of a good-looking man. Late thirties, maybe mid-forties; it was difficult to tell for sure. His dark brown hair had a few strands of silver, and his beard was short and well-groomed. From the angle, I couldn't see much else save he wore a nice black dress shirt. He reminded me a bit of that actor——Jeffrey Dean Morgan——just slightly younger.

"Not a favor. My *ask* for the post-interview," he said cheerfully. "Do you know where The Swill Bar and Grill is?"

I nodded; I hadn't stepped foot in any kind of after-hours place since quitting codeine. My pulse quickened at the thought, but I pushed away the thoughts of the pain-less high that drug gave me. "Near Bank Street, right?"

"That's right." He tapped the photo still in my hands. "You'll go there tonight at ten o'clock and find this man."

My hand trembled, and I lowered it; I didn't want him to know I was scared. "And then what?"

"I'll communicate to you what to do next." He got to his feet, and I bolted upright as well. Not that sitting and standing was much different with his height. He leaned into my space, and I froze. "Dress for the occasion," he said with a chuckle, then left without another word.

I wasn't sure how long I stayed still in the main room of my apartment, but it felt like a ridiculous amount. I grabbed my phone from the coffee table and set an alarm for nine o'clock; I preferred being too early than too late. Especially since I had no idea what would happen if I failed one of his favors——or asks, or whatever he wanted to call them.

With the alarm set, I opened the closet and sifted through the clothes. These were all dresses, but none seemed quite right for a bar and grill. They were either summer dresses or for nightclubs; skimpy. Finally, I picked a dark red one. Sleeveless with a v-shaped opening at my chest and an open slit at the bottom for easier walking. I picked a pair of black high-heeled sandals that matched the color of my hair and put them aside.

It was only five o'clock, and there was plenty of time to linger, though. I decided to eat a frozen meal, putting a second reminder to start my makeup more toward eight. It had been a while since I'd put any on save for the basic, and I knew it would likely take longer than planned.

The whole time I ate, the food tasted stale, as though nothing was quite the same. This wasn't what I expected when I'd dreamed up the scenarios of interviewing him. He was...different than I thought he'd be. And I wasn't sure how to feel about that.

Still tired from the whole ordeal from last night, I curled up into the armchair he'd been sitting in. I rested my head against the back and inhaled his scent. Always wood and musk. The smell enveloped me as I closed my eyes, lulling me into a sense of safety I shouldn't feel.

10

BAIT AND SWITCH

I tugged on the dress again as I got off the bus and headed to my destination. On a Friday night, the streets were bustling in downtown Ottawa. People prepared to bar hop, while others were hanging out with friends.

My eight o'clock alarm had woken me from a restless sleep—something about leather-gloved hands touching me everywhere—and I'd rushed to get ready. Thankfully, the bus wasn't late, so I arrived twenty minutes ahead of time.

My footsteps resonated against the pavement as I went down the stairs to the entrance of the bar. Most people didn't even realize this place existed despite the old flashing sign, which was a shame since it was a lot nicer inside than out. From the outside, it looked like a dive people should avoid.

Music played on the overhead speakers, and I walked past a few groups of people chatting. Booths and tables were occupied by patrons, and although I looked around everywhere, I couldn't spot the man I was here to bait.

As more people flooded in, I checked my phone for

what seemed like the hundredth time. Still no sign of the man. What if there was another bar and grill with the same name? What if I'd gone to the wrong location? My stomach churned at the thought, and I quickly moved toward the exit before slowing down. No. I was panicking for nothing. It wasn't even ten yet; I was early.

Someone grasped my elbow. "I thought I said ten o'clock," the killer's voice said in amusement.

I froze. It was as though all the noise inside the place vanished, and only his words lingered. They seemed to echo around me, and for a second, I was tempted to run for it. If he was here, in public, then he wouldn't be wearing the mask. Did that mean he planned on killing me by the end?

Two men approached, and one put out his hand. The killer shook it, and I continued to stare in a daze.

"Jack. I thought you weren't working tonight," one of the men said. His blond hair fell a bit in front of his baby blue eyes as he shook his hand.

"I'm not," he said as he tugged on my elbow.

The men seemed to get his meaning—one I wanted to clarify—but my mouth seemed to have stopped working.

Jack.

Jack and Jill?

Life had to be kidding.

"Well, enjoy yourselves," the man with the black hair said, waving as they walked away.

Music seemed to pick up even louder, and soon, a group of people danced on the main floor. They were certainly a rowdy bunch.

"You still won't look at me?" Jack asked as though hurt.

I turned toward him, focusing straight ahead at his chest. "If I do... then..." I wasn't sure what would happen. Would I die on the spot?

He pushed a finger under my chin, forcing my head back. It was the man in the photo. The handsome one I was supposed to...

I placed my hand on his chest and took a step back. "Wait. What kind of game are you playing?" I said through gritted teeth. "You said you needed me as bait, so what am I—"

"You're not very patient, are you, darling girl?" His pet name for me seemed to shoot straight down between my thighs, and I pressed my legs together hard. I really hated the effect he had on me. Why was he so good looking, and why was he fucking around with me?

"If this is some fucked up game—"

"Language," he said in a dark tone.

"Fuck. You." I walked past him, but he wrapped an arm around my waist and pulled me close to him.

"Jill," he growled.

Using my name stopped me from elbowing him in the ribs, and instead, I turned in his grasp. Without missing a beat, I wrapped my arms around his neck, and his eyebrows shot up. "What could you possibly do if I left right now? Pull out your..." I glanced down between us, then looked back up at him, batting my eyelashes, "weapon and kill me?"

His smirk was somehow scarier than when he looked annoyed seconds ago. "Don't tempt me." He motioned over my shoulder. "Don't look now, but your real mark is just where you want him."

So he did want to use me as bait but wanted to get seeing him out of the way first. Part of me deflated a little, imagining trying to bait him, of all people. He spun me, pulling me closer to his chest as he leaned in toward my ear. "One of the men who came to say hello... by the bar. You're going to tell him how I was ungentlemanly toward you and how you just want good company for once."

I wasn't sure I breathed as he spoke. He was close. Too close. His smell would be all over me by the end of the night. All I could think of was how I couldn't wait to get home so I could have some alone time with my dildo.

Swallowing hard, I moved to the music with him, then spun back to face him. "Okay, and then what?" I asked in a small voice. Somehow, the thought of disappointing him scared me more than anything else I was about to do.

"Don't worry about it. I'll take care of the rest." He leaned forward, his gaze burning into mine. "Now, look insulted, and walk away."

I gawked at him. "You're such an asshole," I said loudly enough that a few people turned in their direction. Without waiting for his reaction, I strode to the bar, stopping near the man with the blond hair.

"I can't believe some... *men*," I hissed the word through my teeth as though it was a curse.

"Everything alright? Did——?"

"We didn't even get to *what are some of your hobbies*," I said in a mimicking low voice. "No. Straight to have you ever squirted with a man?"

The man nearly choked on his drink; whatever he expected, it wasn't that. "Really? Jack?" he said, eyes wide as he glanced back toward Jack.

I could barely hide my smile as he glared toward me, obviously having heard what I'd said. Too bad. If he was going to play mind games with me, I'd do the same with him.

Yeah, but he'll kill you if you piss him *off too much.*

"What can I say... all men are pigs. Is it too much to ask to get a drink with someone and just... talk?" I asked.

"Larry," the man called out at the bartender, who

made his way toward them. He stared at me and gave me a charming smile. "What'll you have?"

I straightened as though the night was suddenly going my way, but in reality, I wished I was still dancing with Jack. "Rye and coke, please. Thank you."

"I'm Michael," he said, putting out his hand.

"Jill," I said, and instead of shaking my hand, he brought my fingers to his lips and brushed them with a kiss.

The room was suddenly chilly, and I had a strange feeling; it was because of the icy stare Jack was giving Michael. If he was Jack's next victim, I pitied him because Jack wouldn't make his death swift.

"Excuse me a second," I said, pulling out my phone and making a note about asking Jack how he picked his victims. He seemed to hate Michael with a passion, and I wondered why, but right then and there wasn't the time to ask. "Sorry about that. Work stuff."

The rye and Coke arrived as I put away my phone and clicked my purse closed. Michael pushed the drink toward me, and I relaxed a little as I took a gulp of my drink. At least the night wouldn't be dull, thanks to a bit of alcohol. I almost snorted out loud at my own train of thought; Jack would make this anything but boring.

11

___

REWARD

I leaned against the bar as warmth infused my body. A pool of heat seemed to settle between my legs, and I smiled ear to ear as Michael said something. I wasn't listening and, instead, I was thinking about Jack. How would he react if I went over there and kissed him? It didn't seem as impossible as before... Who cared about the ethics of the interview? Why did I even care about my report? In the end, the final result would be the same, wouldn't it? That has always been the plan.

My heart raced at the thought. This wasn't right. A familiar weightlessness filled my body. When had I felt like this before?

"You want to head out?" Michael asked; he was much too close to me. I didn't care for him. Yet my stomach fluttered at the way he looked at me. As though he wanted to fuck me right then and there.

I nodded and giggled, allowing him to lead me toward the exit. But where was Jack? Was I supposed to leave with Michael?

The summer air was hot and sticky. I raised my arms

above my head and twirled a few times, laughing. Life was such a wonderful thing. And if I kept spinning, maybe I'd float away. Michael stopped me, and I pouted as he led me toward a red car. I was buckled in, and he got into the driver's seat then started the engine. Where were we going?

I glanced back, checking to see if I could spot Jack. Should I get out? My head lightened, and I decided against it; I was too comfy to move. The vehicle was warm, but the scents... it was as though everything smelled so good.

He drove for some time, but I didn't mind at all. The lights were so pretty as they passed by. It was as though they all shined on me, and I basked in their spotlights. I lifted my hand and moved my fingers around as they tingled. This was nice.

Michael pulled into a private road, then stopped in an underground parking lot. I tried opening the door to get out, but my limbs were heavy. It was the strangest feeling, but I could only laugh at it.

Thankfully, he was a gentleman and helped me out. I wondered what Jack would've done if it was him. Yanked me from the car, and fucked me on the hood? My pulse throbbed uncontrollably between my legs, and I pressed them together. It was too much. I needed release, but Jack wasn't here. At least back home, I could use my toy and think of him.

"Let's get you inside," Michael said, continuing with his charming manners.

I scoffed as we entered an apartment building. I didn't want to go inside; I wanted someone inside *me*. Preferably Jack.

"First-floor unit?" I asked, my voice sounding far away as he unlocked a door, and we stepped in. I didn't like those; anyone could come in from the windows. Or patio door. It was too easy. I giggled, recalling how I was on the second floor, and Jack had broken in without an issue. Twice. "How *did* he get in?"

"What?" Michael asked as he closed the door behind him.

But before he could lock it, someone kicked it open, hitting him right in the face with a loud crunch. There was a muffled groan and blood, but the rest didn't make sense. I staggered back; it was too loud.

I stared at the familiar black mask as Jack helped me sit on something soft. More moaning was coming from the floor nearby, but I couldn't seem to look away from the killer.

"Sit here and stay," he ordered, and I could only nod.

His scent was intoxicating, and I watched as he readjusted his leather gloves. I wanted him to touch me with them. Maybe he would if I asked?

I leaned back in the seat and opened my legs. "I'm horny..."

He crouched in front of me, his gloved hands caressing my inner thighs. "I know, darling girl, but it won't last much longer. Close your eyes and rest."

"No," I said with a pout.

His hand squeezed against my skin, and I winced. "Do as you're told, and you'll get a reward."

I closed my eyes as an expansive feeling seemed to start in my chest and travel outward, as though my extremities were warm and ready to float away. As I drifted away, sounds caught my ear. I tried listening, but the words were jumbled. There were questions. An answer. There was a lot of muffled screaming. I slid to the side and landed on something soft; was I on a sofa? The fabric was rigid, but at least it was comfy.

A whooshing noise caught my attention, and I squinted

one eye open. If Jack caught me peeking, I wouldn't get a reward, but I was too curious not to look. A blade shone in the light as it blurred out of view, plunging down until it vanished from my sight. Over and over. I watched, mesmerized, as it came up more red than before. The silver started to disappear, instead covered in a crimson liquid that dripped and splattered around.

Did he need help? I tried sitting up, but my body refused to obey. Yet everything else was fine. There was no dull pain. No worries or concerns. Slowly, I let out a small giggle as a flood of realization hit me; I was drugged. And it was okay because it felt good. I staggered to my feet, eyes closed as an overflow of energy seemed to burst through me. It was time to go home. I had to leave.

The scent of wood and copper overwhelmed my senses for a second as strong arms wrapped around my waist. I kept my eyes closed as I breathed him in, as though he carried me away to a world of calm.

"Can you walk on your own?" he asked in a hushed tone.

I nodded, letting out a shuddering breath; his voice did something to my insides I couldn't describe. As though I soaked in his every word.

The smell of the inside of a car. I blinked a few times and frowned. When had I gotten into a vehicle? I was lying in the backseat. Jack drove, still wearing those gloves. That floating feeling didn't go away, so I closed my eyes again and gripped the side of the seat.

Home. Jack locked the door for me—even put the chain—before turning to me. Those black eyeholes watched me. I swallowed hard.

Before I knew it, I had trudged to my bed and let myself fall onto it. The dress rode up past my panties, and I raised my knees, swinging them side to side.

He sat on the edge of my mattress, and I stopped. Was he going to give me the reward he said he would?

"I feel..." I didn't know what. It was a whirlwind of different feelings taking over me. I parted my legs and reached in between, rubbing my fingers against the fabric. "I...need..." I still couldn't find the right words.

He slid his thumb by my soaking entrance, the gloves so warm against my skin, I nearly melted into him. His fingers pushed the panties aside, and he pushed in two fingers in one motion. I arched back and moaned as his knuckles pressed against my clit. With the leather, they seemed so much thicker than I imagined. He thrust in and out in a steady rhythm. I was so wet; they slid in and out with ease.

"You're dripping all over me," he nearly growled, and I clenched around his fingers.

His voice radiated through me, and I whimpered. I lifted my dress higher, and he continued pumping, then pushed up my bra.

"More..." I begged.

"More of this?" He slammed in deeper, and I screamed. I rolled my nipple between my thumb and finger, massaging the other breast as pressure built within.

"Voice," I nearly shouted.

For a second, everything seemed to stop. He hovered over me, the black mask the only inkling it was still him. "Ah, so you enjoy the sound of my voice, darling girl?"

He pushed deeper inside with his fingers, and I could've sworn he'd added a third. He thrusted faster, picking up speed as I continued playing with my breasts and nipples.

"Fuck yes," I moaned. The sound of his voice, along with the mask's breathiness, just made me want to cum so hard.

He pulled out his fingers and slapped my mound. Hard. I squealed as spasms of pleasure filled me. "Language," he warned.

"I'm sorry," I whined, writhing under him.

He pushed back inside, pumping faster and faster until I shuddered uncontrollably around his fingers. Sensual waves caressed me as I seemed to melt into my mattress, closing my eyes.

12

CLOSENESS

*S*unlight filtered through the curtains, and I groaned. I rolled to the side and grimaced at the pounding headache. It wasn't like me to drink to this point. Not anymore.

Everything hurt in a dull ache, and I slowly opened my eyes. My makeup crusted over my eyelashes, and I swore under my breath. Why hadn't I bothered to wash up when I got home?

"Ugh..." I swung my feet over my bed and stared down at my naked body. It felt oddly satisfied in a way I couldn't make sense of. With a shrug, I trudged to the bathroom and closed the door behind me.

The mirror told the story of a drunk who'd regretted her life choices. The mascara had leaked down the side of my face, and my eyeshadow was smudged. I looked like a clown.

The shower was nice, but as I washed my hair, I frowned at the low ache between my legs. Why was I a bit sore? Had I used my dildo the night before? I couldn't recall much of anything.

I grabbed the makeup wipes I'd brought into the shower with me and cleaned off my face. Last night seemed to flash through my mind. Bits and pieces—some blurred—but it all came back. I dropped the pad and gawked at the pipes in front of me, blinking fast. No. That couldn't have happened. I hadn't made a fool of myself.

Pushing my face under the water, I was tempted to try drowning myself. Instead, I took a few steps back, spitting out and trying to breathe again. I could die of embarrassment.

I got out of the shower and dried off as I continued fighting against the nausea. What had I been drugged with, anyway? From what I recalled, all the pain—physical and mental—had vanished, and it was as though I'd been floating. It was like codeine but without the drowsiness.

At the thought, my skin crawled. No. I'd worked so hard to get rid of the cravings, and it was as though I started at square one again. The air was suddenly cold, so I grabbed the robe hanging behind the door and slipped it on before heading back out.

"Good morning," Jack said from the armchair.

I yelped, "Fucking hell."

He turned in his seat and shot me a dark look. "One of these days, I'm going to wash your mouth out with soap."

"How long have you been sitting there?" I asked, ignoring his comment and trying even harder to ignore the way he looked at me.

He rubbed his face with his hand as he got to his feet, his beard bristling. "All night. Wanted to make sure you didn't end up throwing up and choking."

Part of me wanted to cry at how considerate that was; no one had ever done something like that for me before. Tears blurred my vision, but I blinked them away as fast as I could. He approached me, but I took a few steps back.

That didn't seem to deter him. If anything, he reached me in seconds and grasped my chin, keeping me in place.

"Why are you crying?"

I wiped at my cheeks, surprised tears had managed to fall; I wasn't usually a crier. "It's nothing."

He tilted my head back, his gaze boring into me. "Don't lie."

I wrenched away from him and took a few more steps back until I hit the wall. "I'm just... This is the third time I've been drugged in two nights. I don't appreciate it, okay? It took forever for me to get off codeine, and now..." I shook my head and let out a sigh. "What did Michael drug me with anyway?"

"It's known as Liquid Ecstasy," he said in a softer tone than before.

"Fan-fucking-tastic," I muttered, knowing all too well what that drug was used for. "What... Did you kill him?"

"I did." He took a few steps closer. "Does that bother you?"

"No." I motioned to the front entrance. "Mind if I take some notes?"

He moved to the side and motioned for me to go ahead. It was strange to see him without his mask or gloves, although the thought of those made my recall the night before a little too vividly. My cheeks heated as I walked past him, but he grasped my arm, stopping me in my steps.

"You never told me."

I arched an eyebrow as I glanced from his hand to his face. "Told you what?"

"The question I apparently asked you last night. Whether or not you've squirted while being with a man." He pushed a strand of my hair behind my ear, and I shivered. "Well... did I make you squirt?"

I muttered several curse words under my breath as I marched away from him. "Please don't remind me of that. I'm already mortified as it is." I grabbed my messenger back and rummaged through my things until I found my notebook.

"Why? Do you have any regrets?"

"Regrets? I'm supposed to keep things ethical... Professional, and I——"

"You were drugged and horny."

I turned to face him. If it wasn't for Jack, I knew what Michael had planned to do to me. The realization seemed to hit me all at the same time, and I burst into tears. I barely raised my hands to my face before Jack held me against his chest, just letting me cry. Between him murdering someone when I was in the same room to staying awake all night to make sure I'd be okay, my emotions were a mess.

For a split second, I wondered if Jack had taken advantage of me considering my drugged state, but I dismissed that thought faster than it appeared. I'd wanted him to touch me before the drug was in my system. But it was done, and I had to stop it while I was ahead.

I backed away, drying my face with the back of my hand as I mumbled apologies. Before he could say anything, I grabbed my notebook from the bag and made my way to the counter island. Once down on the surface, I opened it, ready to start taking notes again.

"Why did you kill Michael? Why him?" I asked, then stared back at Jack.

His expression was stony, and for a moment, he almost looked as though he wouldn't answer. "Why not?" he asked.

"Well, for one thing, he seemed to know you. I didn't think you'd murder someone who could be connected to you." I noted down Jack's reluctance to answer questions this time.

"I work as a bouncer at several nightclubs and a few bars." He shrugged. "Michael was a regular, so he eventually caught my name."

No wonder he was so muscular—if he had to throw people out for being too rowdy, carrying me back into my apartment was probably a bit easier for him than most.

"But you killed him almost right after Patrice... Don't you usually wait about a month?"

He chuckled as he approached, one hand in his pants pocket as though he was taking a leisurely stroll. "You believe you've discovered some sort of pattern with the way I kill?"

It was almost a challenge.

"Usually, it's around once a month, isn't it?" I asked, flipping back through my previous notes. I took out a few of the crime scene photos I'd printed out and laid them across the counter.

"And where did you get these?" he asked in a curious tone.

"A classmate of mine, Trevor, works for the Ottawa Police Department. He took some photos of the evidence for me."

Jack frowned. "Why would he risk his job and jail time to do that?"

"Because men like blowjobs."

He walked around the counter, and I stiffened to keep from backing away. "I see." He grabbed the side of my neck, his thumb tracing along my throat as I swallowed hard. "Don't do it again."

My eyebrows shot up, and I wondered if he meant doing something illegal or giving blowjobs. "All men or just Trevor?"

"Whichever ones you don't want dead," he said darkly.

I pushed his hand away and put my hands on my hips. Looking authoritative was difficult when he stared at me hungrily, though. And when he stood so much taller.

"Look. I'm sorry about what happened last night and me crying just now. It won't happen again. But this"—I motioned between the two of us—"is supposed to be an ethical relationship. I ask questions, you answer."

He smiled, but it didn't reach his eyes. "And you give me my ask of the day."

"Glad we're clear on that, then." But I had the feeling it was anything but clear.

13

A GIFT

With the regular semester back in full swing, I barely had time for any interviews. Not that it mattered since I hadn't seen Jack for the past week. The last time was when I'd tried making our relationship clear. Was he angry with me about that? I scoffed at the thought; it wouldn't make any sense for him to be upset in the first place.

The weather was still hot, but the nights slowly began cooling down. Every time I returned home, part of me expected Jack to be inside my apartment, but he never was.

Elsie came rushing in for our afternoon class, late as usual, and plopped down right next to me. "Have you heard?" Elsie whispered.

I shushed her, motioning to the professor, who shot us a dirty look; the class only had around twenty students, so it wasn't as though we wouldn't be noticed.

"Sorry, Professor, but it's about Trevor," Elsie said as tears filled her eyes. "Didn't you hear?"

Professor Santor's solemn expression churned my stomach, but I didn't dare believe something actually happened to him. It couldn't be. "Yes. I heard this morning. The police came to speak with me since he attended this class..." He let out a sigh as he shook his head. "For those who don't know, one of the students here, Trevor Sullivan, was unfortunately killed in a fire last night."

"A fire?" Another student repeated. "Where? I don't remember hearing anything about——"

"It was in a Chinatown apartment," Elsie chimed in. "The restaurant downstairs caught fire, and the flames took the whole building in a matter of minutes."

If I was drawn to serial killers, Elsie was definitely curious about arson. We weren't exactly friends since I was older than her—and the majority of my peers—by five years.

"For those who need to talk to someone, I'll be here after class," the professor continued, "and there are always the many programs available to students, for free, for any mental health needs." He turned his back to the class and started writing the study material for today on the whiteboard.

My mind was reeling. "I can't believe it..." I muttered. Trevor was just... gone? Yet, it shouldn't surprise me; everyone I was around seemed to die from the time I was born. It was as though death wanted me all to itself.

The rest of the class seemed to pass in a strange blur, but soon enough, the clock hand moved, and Professor Santor dismissed us.

"Want to grab a coffee and go over the notes?" Elsie asked with a grin as we walked outside.

"Sure." I was still a bit in a daze as we went to our favorite coffee shop. I knew Elsie needed the notes from the start of the period, and I wasn't opposed to sharing. "Why were you late this time?"

"I went to see what was left of the building after the fire," she said, as though it was obvious.

"That's not morbid at all." I was definitely one to talk.

"If you heard a serial killer murdered someone inside a building, you'd rush there hoping for a photo op or something," Elsie shot back with a grin. She sobered quickly as we approached the shop. "I can't believe he's dead, though. Apparently, the kitchen staff didn't turn off one of their old stoves properly, and there'd been oil left behind. Place was old, so it just burned down fast."

I ordered an iced white mochaccino and joined Elsie at one of the tables where she was already busy copying the missed notes. We studied, exchanging notes about the subject—human rights in journalism—and after a couple of hours, I stretched.

"I think I'm going to call it a day," I said, grabbing my books and notes, then putting them back into my messenger bag. "Any plans this weekend?"

"Spending what little time I have with my boyfriend while he's off work. I hate that he has to work shifts most days."

"Well, enjoy your time together," I said with a small wave as I left the shop.

It was already a bit cooler outside, and I couldn't help but let out a sigh. So many of my classmates had partners despite being younger than me. I usually didn't mind, but sometimes, it was lonely. Not that it would matter in eight months. After my report was finished, so was I.

I approached my building and eyed it. The place was old; would it burn down quickly like Trevor's apartment had? Burning to death wasn't exactly the way I wanted to go. I stepped inside, and the smell of mold caught my nose. I grimaced; this place couldn't burn down with how humid it was.

As I got to my door, I frowned at a small box left in front of it. I hadn't ordered anything... Maybe it was delivered to the wrong address?

I unlocked the door, then picked it up before heading inside. It was a bit stuffier inside since I'd turned off my air conditioner and left the window open instead. Still, I wouldn't complain since, soon enough, I'd be bitching about all the snow.

Why couldn't I live somewhere that was always autumn?

The box weighed nothing, and I opened it, kicking off my sandals at the same time. Something beige and red was inside a sealed plastic bag, and my eyes widened as I backed away from it.

It couldn't be real. I had to be imagining things. It was because of the news about Trevor; my mind was playing tricks on me. I peeked inside again, swallowing hard. It wasn't fake. That was a real dismembered...*member*.

"Oh fuck..." I grabbed the piece of paper stuck between the cardboard and plastic with a shaky hand and opened it.

Trevor screamed when I removed it.

I dropped the note, and the world around me seemed to spin for a few seconds. No. He... hadn't. A knock at the door pulled me out of my panic, and I quickly looked through the peephole.

"Think of the devil, and he'll appear," I muttered through gritted teeth. I opened the door, and Jack leaned against the frame with a grin.

"Hello, Jill."

I grabbed his t-shirt and wrenched him inside—although he likely wanted to come in, or I wouldn't have been able to just force him—then slammed the door shut. Pacing didn't help, so I pointed at the box.

"What the fuck is this?" I nearly shouted.

His jaw clenched. "What—"

"If you tell me to watch my language, I swear to god, I'll..." I left the rest hanging, unsure what to threaten a serial killer with.

"I decided to remove the temptation to have any further intimacy with him."

My hands curled into fists. "Temptation? What do you see me as? A whore?"

"You wanted something, and he took advantage of you for it," he said, taking a step forward. "I taught him a valuable lesson before he died."

Part of me wanted to scream, but another part—a more messed up one—desperately wanted to take my notebook out and write this down.

I let out a breath, trying to calm down as I pointed at the box. "What if someone had stolen this?"

"I waited until you left the coffee shop before leaving it at your door."

The silence seemed to take a form of its own as he stared at me with darkness behind his gaze.

"You were... Have you been stalking me?"

"I've been checking up on you when I feel it necessary. Is that so odd, considering you have my life in your hands?"

"*Your* life?" I repeated loudly. But the more I thought about it, the more I realized he was right to a certain degree. I trusted him not to kill me just as much as he trusted me not to identify him to the authorities. Which was likely not very much on either side.

I raised my hands in surrender. "Okay, okay. I'm not going to argue with you about that since it wasn't a condition I ever put in place." I shot him a glare. "My mistake, apparently."

"So do you not like my gift?" he asked with a smirk.

"No more killing people I know."

"No promises," he said with a wink.

My heart hammered against my chest as I held his gaze. "Please, Jack."

He stared at me for a few seconds as though debating whether or not to agree, but the ghost of a smile touched his lips and he nodded. "Alright."

I could only hope he'd keep his word.

14

———

OPENING

"**I** have a big favor to ask," I said as I closed my notebook.

"Oh? Are we exchanging roles today?" Jack asked in amusement. "I interview you, and you have an *ask* of me?"

I thought about it for a few seconds, surprised that's what he'd want in exchange. "I mean... if that's what you want. But you don't even know what the favor is yet."

"Then ask," he said, motioning toward me to go ahead.

I bit my lower lip, wondering how exactly I could go about asking this. "I'd like to shadow you. See what you do on a regular day. And then maybe I could follow you on a day you kill someone to see if it differs in any way..."

"A regular day I'm off or one where I'm working my job?" he asked, not looking fazed by my request.

He didn't seem reluctant, and I buzzed with excitement. "Both if you're comfortable."

"That's a big ask." He got to his feet and sat on the coffee table in front of me. His leg pushed up between mine, forcing them apart a little. "I get to ask you a big question, then. And remember...I want the truth."

I swallowed hard and nodded. "Okay..."

"Did you have a good childhood?" he asked with a grin.

My eyebrows shot up, not at all expecting him to use my first question to him on me. I chose my words carefully, though. "My aunt raised me. She was a great mom and always showed me a lot of love."

"What happened to your biological parents?" He took out his knife and began picking at his fingernails. It was as though he was giving me the space to answer without him staring at me, which I appreciated.

"I was born prematurely... spent the first few months of my life in the neonatal intensive care unit." It was strange recounting the story to him, allowing him a glimpse into a life I'd long put into the past. "The doctor recommended my parents go home to spend time with my brother... you know, show him his parents were still there and cared." I let out a long breath, and he stared up at me. "They decided to bring my brother to the hospital to see me, but they never made it back. It was snowing that day, and there was an accident. All three died in a car crash."

He pushed the tip of the blade under my chin. "Is that why you have a fascination with death?"

"Something like that," I said with a smirk as I placed my finger against the blade and pushed it away. "I just..."

"What?"

"I often wonder how I would've turned out if that accident never happened. Parents and a brother... it seems so weird to think of." I laughed, waving my hand dismissively. "It doesn't matter, though. My aunt was a wonderful mom, and she raised me with a lot of love. Can't complain."

His gaze searched mine for a few seconds as though trying to figure out if I was lying or hiding something. In my case, it was definitely the latter, but as far as his question went, I'd answered truthfully. Technically.

"Did you ever attend therapy to talk about all those little *what-ifs*?" he asked.

My defenses rose, and I bristled. "Of course I did," I snapped. "What about you?"

He chuckled. "You already know the answer to that. It's why you went to see Professor Frauley. Didn't you get my patient file?"

"Well...most of it was redacted for privacy reasons," I said quietly. It had been one thing to look through someone's file when he was just a serial killer, but it was something else entirely to have read through some of the keywords left behind in the notes when I was speaking with the man. "Was that the only time you had therapy? In your early twenties?"

"Yes." He tapped his knife against his chin, still surveilling me, then put it away. "Thank you for answering my question."

"Did you take your weapon out to stop me from lying or something?" I asked with a smirk.

His eyes darkened. "If you had lied and invented a story, things may have turned out differently just now."

"And how do you know for sure I didn't?" I asked quietly; I wasn't sure why I'd instigate him into doubting me, but I was too curious not to ask.

He smiled, but it didn't reach his eyes. "You're easier to read than you think."

I scoffed; part of me wanted to tell him I obviously wasn't since he hadn't picked up on the fact I was, in fact, hiding a bit more. Using his question's specifics didn't count as lying, but I knew better. I was definitely playing with fire.

He got to his feet and walked toward the entrance. I followed his movements, then caught sight of the box again.

"What card did he choose?" The words blurted out of my mouth before I realized what I'd said. Instantly, I stiffened as he narrowed his eyes on me. His jaw clenched as he came back, but instead of sitting in front of me, he stood behind me. He grasped my shoulders and leaned down by the side of my face.

"And how would you know about that?" he asked, not hiding the hint of fury in his tone.

I swallowed several times, trying to get my mouth to work. He squeezed tighter, and I winced.

"It's how I connected specific murders to you. It's why you don't have a set way to kill people... you actually have four. Sometimes, five."

His hand wrapped around my throat, and I grasped his wrist as he put pressure. "You have one minute to explain exactly what you know, or I'll show you how easy it is to choke someone and bring them back over and over," he growled in my ear.

I did my best to ignore how my body reacted to that threat and pointed toward where my kitchen table was. "It's in my files. I can show you." It was as though I was running a race with how fast I was panting. Little black spots appeared in my vision, and he released me just as I was feeling weightless.

With a gasp, I leaned forward, away from him, and massaged my neck. I got to my feet, narrowing my eyes at him as I went to the opened box sitting on the chair. It was where I kept the files I'd gotten throughout my years of collecting evidence. I pulled a file out and flipped through to make sure it was the right one.

"Here..." I yelped when I came face to face with him—or rather, to his chest with how tall he was—and nearly dropped the file. "You really need to stop sneaking up on me. You're going to give me a heart attack." When he didn't move, I sighed and grabbed the photos from the folder, spreading them across the table.

He stared at them, then back at me, anger still dancing behind his gaze. "You have around thirty seconds left."

I rolled my eyes as I picked up one of the photos and pointed at a particular spot. "Every single one of these pictures has a deck of playing cards in them. Some were brought into evidence because there were blood splatters on them. The ones that were brought in, I was able to ask about or look into myself, and one of the jacks was always missing."

He gave a condescending smile. "And you figured that out with just this?"

"I did. Took years, but I eventually put two and two together." I raised my head higher in defiance.

He grabbed my throat, and my eyes widened. "You said *five* different ways."

"The Joker. It was missing twice..."

"And what," he pulled me closer, so we were almost nose to nose, "is your theory about that?"

"When your victim refuses to choose, you pick for them with a Joker."

"I knew you were clever, but you're even more fascinating than I thought."

"Thank you?" I breathed, unsure if he was still angry or not. I decided to push my luck a bit. "So, what are each card's options?"

The ghost of a smile touched his lips as he let me go. He pulled out a deck of cards, opening the box and letting them fall into his hands. My heart hammered against my chest as he grabbed the four Jacks and held them up.

"Why don't you pick one and find out?"

15

———

CARDS

"Spade," I said, already guessing it would have to do with using a knife.

Each kill was different, depending on the jack type the victims chose, but sometimes, the bodies were maimed beyond belief, and the cause of death was difficult to determine.

Jack motioned for me to take the card, and I did, holding it against my chest as though it might protect me from him. "That one is stabbing."

I was about to ask about the others but if he'd wanted to tell me, he would've. "Now what?"

"You hold onto that card for now... until the time calls for it," he said with a cold smile that sent shivers down my spine. He motioned at the photos scattered across the table. "Were these the only ones you found?"

I gawked at him. "How many more are there?"

"Is that an interview question?" he asked in mock surprise. "No, no. Your next task is to shadow me next week, so that means you get to observe only."

I opened and closed my mouth, wanting to argue, but I

decided against it. I'd pushed my luck with him a few times, and I wasn't about to push more. Especially at the risk he'd change his mind and refuse to let me follow him.

"In the meantime," he said, grabbing a fistful of my hair, and bending me over onto the table. "Which is your favorite victim of mine?" He leaned forward, pushing against me. "What photo speaks to you?" he asked with a chuckle.

I squirmed but froze when something hard pressed against my ass. "They're all interesting because they each tell a story," I said through gritted teeth. He was enjoying this way too much, and the biggest problem was that I was, too.

"Is that so?" He trailed his fingers along my back, and I trembled. "How about I tell you what the other cards are in exchange for an ask of my own?"

I knew what the favor would be this time, and I wasn't opposed. Even though I really should be. But it was for the sake of my report; this would give my confirmation on which card meant what. No matter what, I had to accept.

"Can I...get my notebook?" I asked tentatively. If he said yes, would he put me back in this position again?

He scoffed and moved away from me. Before I could straighten, he pushed back against me and placed a pen into my hand. "Use the back of one of the photos."

"And what's...your ask?" I asked in a whisper.

The table creaked as he leaned his hands on either side of me. "You're going to write them down while I fuck you."

I turned my head to the side, eyebrows rising so high, I was sure they'd vanished. "Language," I said in a mocking tone.

The table creaked again, and he slapped the side of my ass with such force, I buried my face into my arm to scream. That fucking asshole had the nerve to punish me for something he did to me constantly. I was going to let him have it. Not then and there, but at some point. When I could think clearly.

He lifted my dress, and my hand trembled as I grabbed one of the pictures and flipped it upside down. The sound of his belt unbuckling sent my pulse shooting south, and then his zipper being pulled down was almost my undoing.

How was he able to turn me on so violently with just everyday sounds?

He pulled down my shorts and panties in one hard tug, and I stiffened as something thick pressed at my center. I did my best to write which card I already knew, but my hand trembled from intensity as he sheathed himself inside me.

I pushed my forehead against the surface as I moaned. God, he felt so good.

"The jack of heart is also done with a knife," he said in a roughly seductive voice. He moved harder into me as something cool and sharp pressed against my neck, and I whimpered. "Want to guess?"

"Slicing...throat," I panted, raising my hips.

"Write it." He bit out the words, and I did as he ordered. The writing was almost illegible with how hard he pounded into me.

"Jack...of clubs?" I asked in quick and hollow breaths. "Is... Ah!" He reached beneath me, his fingers circling my clit.

"Choking, yes." He grunted as though satisfied, and for a second, I worried he was already finished. Instead, he leaned forward again, thrusting in deeper. He shoved his fingers into my mouth, and I tasted myself. "Diamond is drowning."

A wave of desire spread out from my chest as I sucked

on them, my heart beating so hard, I thought it would explode. He grabbed my hips, pulled out almost completely, and then slammed into me over and over as I screamed. Writing was impossible, but every time I tried to stop, he slapped my ass in warning. It stung, and tears blurred my vision, and I did my best to write it all down.

"And Joker...is *my* choice." He pumped into me harder, the sound of wet slapping filling the room. He bucked within me and hissed through his teeth. "*Mine.*"

I cried out in a wild eruption of pleasure, the singular world bringing me over the edge. I let myself fall forward onto the table, gasping in short little spurts. My hand trembled as I wrote the last card's option, letting out a tiny cry as he pulled out of me. I suddenly felt so empty. And my ass throbbed like hell.

To my surprise, he lifted me into his arms and carried me to the sofa where he held me close to him. My emotions seemed to come back down from a high I'd never experienced before. I wanted to say something, but no words seemed to form. Instead, I closed my eyes and cuddled up to him. Wood, musk, and sex. I could get used to this.

For as long as possible, anyway.

16

HOME

*E*xcitement bubbled to the surface, and I double-checked a few times to make sure I hadn't forgotten anything. Three days and three nights I'd be spending shadowing Jack to see what his day-to-day life looked like.

I'd be able to write all about the differences in a day when he worked versus when he had the day off. And depending on if he'd actually allow me to see what happened when he murdered someone. My final report would benefit so much from these experiences, and I couldn't wait.

As I grabbed my duffle bag with my change of clothes, notebook, and other basic necessities, I headed outside. It was finally starting to cool down as the month progressed, and soon enough, I expected the leaves to change colors. I couldn't wait; red, oranges, and yellows painted by nature. It was always so beautiful.

Jack leaned against a car, waiting. It wasn't the same vehicle as last time. I almost asked how many he owned, but I'd promised to wait until we got to his place before asking too many questions. Instead, I walked up to him, beaming.

"Hey," I said. It was strange to be peppy near someone who could so easily kill me. And who would if it wasn't for the PIN I had to keep inputting every evening. At the thought that the PIN was the only reason, my heart sank a bit, but I pushed it aside quickly. It didn't matter if he liked me or not; that wasn't the point of my report. Besides, relationships were messy and useless.

He opened the trunk and took the bag from me. "Good afternoon, Jill."

The way he said my name always sent butterflies fluttering inside my stomach. I hated it felt so nice. I was supposed to be a professional. He was supposed to be a stone-cold killer. And instead, he played mind games with me, going from threatening me to fucking in a matter of seconds. Often at the same time.

We drove off, and the ride was silent. Not uncomfortable or awkward, but pleasant. I hadn't been in this part of the city since taking a bus would take forever, so I was enjoying the sights. Soon enough, it became more industrial, with warehouses every few buildings. The few apartment buildings were either decrepit or brand new and looked as though they cost thousands per month. Which was ridiculous considering how far we were from downtown.

He pulled into a parking lot with a singular building. It looked like a small warehouse with one floor, but he continued straight down into an underground garage. The door opened after he pushed a button on his cellphone, and then he drove inside. My pulse sped as darkness swallowed us, save for the headlights.

Electricity buzzed overhead, and lights switched on as he put the car in park. "We're here."

It was strange being back, considering the last time I arrived and left, I'd been sedated. This time, he was allowing me to see where he lived. Allowing me into his space. He unlocked the only door, and music filtered through; classical.

The place was amazing and not at all what I pictured. Although it had been difficult for me to really imagine anything, considering he'd put me in a tiny empty room the first time I'd been here. The place was built like a studio apartment but huge. Stone walls on either end held more paintings than I could count and of all sizes. The kitchen was large, with several counters and overhead cupboards. Did he like to cook?

"Bedroom area is there," he said as he rolled up his sleeves. He motioned to a nook inside the wall where a king bed rested, curtains opened on either side. I couldn't help but envy him; that looked like such a comfortable place to sleep; a four-poster bed, but with mostly walls instead.

A sofa, loveseat, and armchair faced toward a flat-screen television with a few consoles below. Easels of all sizes stood around the room, some with unfinished paintings.

"You paint?" I asked as I approached one that looked finished. "It's beautiful."

The portrait of a woman looking to the sky as swans flew past her. Delicate and innocent. So unlike him. Not that I'd say it, but writing it all down came to mind as I took everything in.

"Thank you." He placed his hand on the side of my hip, leading me farther into the room, past the kitchen. "It keeps me busy."

I understood the unspoken words: until he had the urge to kill again.

On the other end of the area, there was a single door next to what looked like a large elevator visible through the freight door. I reminded myself that this place was likely once a warehouse, so it would make sense for this to be here. "You have downstairs neighbors?" I asked in surprise.

He shook his head. "The building belongs to me. I live alone."

I almost asked how he was able to afford it but decided to try keeping my questions to a bare minimum; I was here to observe for the time being.

He motioned at the singular door. "That's the washroom." He lifted the freight door and shot me a grin. "Curious about the basement?"

I nodded, my pulse throbbing in my ears as I wondered what would be down there. A torture room? Dungeon? I recalled the empty room I had been shackled in. Was that it?

We stepped inside, and after inserting a key into a hole in the control panel, it went down. My heart seemed to lodge itself into my throat with how fast it went down, and I quickly grabbed on to the nearest thing. Which happened to be his arm.

He didn't comment, but I still let go. I needed to find a way to put a wedge between us; this couldn't have a happy ending.

He opened the freight door, and I stepped out. It wasn't at all what I imagined. A few bookcases lined the wall, and two large shelves with various items were pushed against a smaller wall to the side. An old clawfoot bathtub stood to the side, barrels sitting nearby. I swallowed hard at the old industrial-type fire pit at the end of the room.

"Where was the room you kept me?" I asked, unable to take my eyes off the white and gray ashes at the bottom of the pit.

He picked up one of the bookshelves as though it weighed nothing, revealing a door. He opened it and shot me an amused look as I stared inside. A single cot with a chain bolted to the wall and a chair in the corner.

"Home sweet home?" he cooed in my ear.

I stiffened, half-expecting him to throw me inside. "Do you often lock people up in here?"

"Only the ones I don't want found." His voice had turned dark as though he was picturing the people he'd murdered then and there.

"And what... do you do to them?" My voice seemed to grow smaller with each question. Did I want to know?

Of course! I need to be taking notes!

He grabbed the back of my neck and led me toward the bathtub. "They get to pick their card, but when they're dead, I soak their bodies in lye."

"Lye?" I repeated with a frown. I'd imagined he'd use some sort of acid.

"It's sodium hydroxide. Mix it with water, and eventually, the only thing left are fragile bones I turn into dust." He gave me a cruel smile. "Those art pieces you think are beautiful... The paint was made using those ashes."

"Oh." It was the only word that came to mind as I stared back at the barrels, likely the lye. "Do you ever...murder people by just forcing them into the tub while they're still alive?"

He scoffed. "I'm a serial killer. Not a monster."

His words weighed heavily on me for a few seconds. "Do you ever deviate from the cards when you choose for them?"

His hand slid around to my throat, and he held me against his chest. "You mean, do I ever just snap their necks and make it quick?" His fingers grasped my chin.

"It's so easy to snuff out a human life. Just one quick move and...it's all over."

"Do you ever do it that way?"

"Sometimes...but it's too fast, in my opinion."

So you are a bit of a monster...

17

JEALOUSY

I changed into my little black dress, the rustling of the material echoing in the immense washroom. Jack could easily have split this room in three and gotten himself a washroom and two more rooms. Still, I had to admit the huge shower with multiple sprays looked inviting. The large counter had one sink, and the toilet was a standard one; nothing too special about those. Although, the space made my bathroom back home look miniature.

I was relieved there was no bathtub in here since my mind was already fixated on the one in the basement. Would he show me what it looked like when he put a body in there? A shiver shot down my back, and I did my best to finish my makeup. Not too much since I wasn't going to the nightclub to party, but I wanted to fit in at least a little.

I stepped out of the washroom and back into the main area. Jack strode forward, slipping on a black t-shirt with the word *security* written beneath the logo of the club. He stopped in his tracks, his gaze raking my body.

"You look ravishing," he said in a husky breath. He

closed the gap between us, then slid his finger along my chest until it stopped in the collar dip of my dress.

"Thank you." I swallowed hard at the way he looked at me. As though he wanted to devour me where I stood. And in that moment, I wasn't sure I'd mind.

Reminding myself I was supposed to keep this professional, I quickly took a step back, clutching my purse against my abdomen. "You look pretty good yourself," I said with a smile.

He dropped his hand, and for a split second, I thought I saw a gleam in his eyes. "Thanks." He went to the door that led to the garage and opened it. "My shift starts in around thirty minutes. We should head out. Have everything you need?"

I glanced into my bag, making sure I had my notebook and pen, then nodded. "All set."

It didn't take as long to get back downtown since there was barely any traffic at seven o'clock in the evening. He parked in a staff-only space, and we got out of the vehicle. It was hotter than the days before, and I welcomed it since I'd be outside for most of the night.

A line formed in front of the club, and we walked past until we reached the entrance.

"Jack, finally here," the man at the door boomed. He wore the same t-shirt as Jack but was a bit shorter, although bulkier. The flashing lights overhead reflected against his shaven head as he grinned. "Thought you were going to leave me high and dry tonight."

"Never." Jack motioned to the man. "This is David Beauchamp." He turned to his co-worker. "David, this is my darling girl, Jill."

My whole body seemed to combust as I shook David's hand. All the while, Jack watched the exchange with narrowed eyes. "Nice to meet you," I said, hoping the night hid a bit of my blush.

"Same." David nudged Jack in the ribs with his elbow before grabbing someone's ID and letting them in after collecting the entrance fee. "Come on in."

Jack grabbed a stool and placed it where one of the doors was kept locked so people couldn't enter that way. "Here." He helped me up, and I wished I wouldn't feel so hot and bothered.

"Why...did you introduce me like that?" I almost hissed.

He arched an eyebrow. "Should I have told him why you're really here?"

I opened and closed my mouth, trying to find an argument, but none came to mind. My shoulders slumped; of course he didn't really think of me as anything else. He just had to find a way to introduce me. "Well, you could've warned me."

He just grinned. "I have to go clock in. David here will keep you safe in the meantime."

"You know this isn't my first time at a nightclub, right? I can take care of myself."

He leaned close so his lips brushed against my ear. "Judging by the favors you were exchanging and the drug addiction you used to have, I don't doubt that at all."

I lifted my hand, wanting nothing better than to smack him, but he grasped my wrist before I even swung. He pulled back a bit, darkness swimming behind his brown eyes as he stared at me. "But things are different now. No one touches you because if they do, you'll get a lot more gifts inside boxes from me. Understand?"

My eyebrows shot up, and I just nodded before he kissed the top of my head and vanished inside the club.

David let a few more people inside, then turned to me

as I took my notebook out. "Was this his idea of a date?" he asked with a laugh.

"No. Just wanted to hang around him while he worked. I can study in the meantime."

"You're a student?" He eyed me as though unsure what kind of student I was and whether he should call the cops.

"Doing my master's degree at uOttawa."

Another few IDs checked, and he nodded. "That's impressive. Never thought I'd see Jack with someone. He always ignores all the people who flirt with him."

The thought of people flirting with him infuriated me. Not that it should since we weren't a thing and never would be, but just... I didn't like it. But I was relieved to hear he usually ignored them.

Was I a special case, then? Or maybe he just never flirted with the patrons... maybe he had sex often. I nearly groaned out loud at my own stupidity; I hadn't even made sure he'd used a condom when we'd fucked. I'd had my tubes tied five years ago, but that didn't protect against STIs.

Jack came back outside, and I busied myself with writing all the information I'd gathered since he'd brought me to his home. From the upstairs to the basement. And from the paintings to the bathtub. I trembled at the thought but did my best to keep my emotions out of it.

Hours passed, and from time to time, I'd glance up to see how Jack acted with others. He was professional, almost never smiling despite the number of women who did, in fact, flirt with him. I wanted to throw *them* in Jack's tub.

"Go take your break and pay attention to your girl," David said while slapping Jack on the back.

Jack gave a curt nod, then turned to me. I slid off the stool and lost my footing, my legs having gone numb. He caught me and helped me stand as I winced. I hadn't even noticed, but now it was as though they were filled with the static of a television.

"Sorry about that," I said, trying to pull away, but he just held me closer.

"I get my meal break. Come on." He wrapped an arm around my waist, and we walked inside the club. The music blared as rowdy people screamed, bouncing around to the beat. Despite the crowd, he managed to push through with ease. The lights flashed from white to red, occasionally plunging the place in an eerie glow.

We pushed past people until we got to the back door and entered an employee's only room.

"Am I allowed in here?" I asked, biting my lower lip.

"Don't worry about it." He pulled me inside, and all the sounds went back to being muffled.

We sat at a table, but instead of sitting across, he took the seat next to me. He grabbed one of the menus and handed it to me.

"What would you like to eat?"

"Oh..." I glanced at the prices, and my stomach dropped; I knew after-hour places were more expensive, but this was ridiculous. "I didn't—"

"Whatever I order is covered on my tab, so don't worry about money if that's what you're about to say." He pointed at the name of a sandwich. "I recommend this if you enjoy Montreal smoked meat."

My mouth watered at the thought. I almost joked I'd prefer his meat but pressed my lips together and just nodded. He got up, then walked back out. The techno music blasted for a second before the door shut again.

We finished eating, and I sighed, leaning back and rubbing my abdomen. "I haven't eaten this much in... well, ever," I said with a giggle. I got to my feet and grabbed both plates before making my way to the sink.

"You don't need to——"

"I don't mind. Need to stretch my legs, anyway." I motioned to him. "You're the one who was standing for hours... getting flirted with the whole time."

He straightened in his seat. "And ignoring their advances."

"I know," I said, finishing washing the dishes. But the audacity of some people. He was working. Flirting was unacceptable. I hated the sting of jealousy, especially when it didn't make any sense.

"Do you ever have sex with any of them?" I blurted out the words before I really thought of what I was asking.

Way to stay professional.

He stood and walked toward me slowly, as though he was taking a leisurely stroll. "And are you asking for yourself personally or to write in that notebook of yours?" Although his voice was calm, nothing about his gaze was; a storm brewed behind them.

"Both," I breathed.

With only a foot separating us, I had to arch back to look up at him.

"My *hobbies* relax me. If I need something more, I pay for it."

"You mean sex workers?" I asked, surprised; I expected him to take the dozens of offers he'd gotten tonight alone.

He nodded. "And I pay extra because I have specific needs and wants." He added, "And yes, I always use protection."

I really wanted to write all this down but made mental notes along the way, not wanting to break the moment. He didn't always want to share, and I wasn't about to interrupt him.

"I imagine it comes as no surprise to you that I enjoy inflicting pain." He grabbed a fistful of my hair and yanked my head back.

I gasped, wincing as each hair pulled against my scalp. "Not even a little," I bit out the words.

He chuckled and let me go before turning back toward the entrance. "I rarely need that, though. The rest keeps me more than satisfied." He glanced over his shoulder at me, hunger dancing behind his eyes as he stared.

I swallowed hard.

18

FURY

$\mathcal{I}$ walked inside the main area, stretching my arms above my head as I let out a yawn. "I don't know how you do these late nights."

"I slept this afternoon." Jack eyed me wearily. "Didn't *you?*"

"Couldn't. Too excited." I quickly added, "To take notes while I observed."

He chuckled, but didn't comment as he pulled off his t-shirt. This time, I got a better look at his bare chest, and I did my best not to stare too much. But it was hard. And so were his muscles.

"Are you hungry?" he asked, making his way to the kitchen and opening the refrigerator. "I have leftover beef stew I made from yesterday."

I couldn't remember the last time I had a home-cooked meal; I usually bought frozen dinners. "I'd love some, thanks." I beamed at him, bouncing on my tiptoes. "I'll just go get cleaned up real quick."

He nodded, and I grabbed my duffle bag on the way to the washroom. Getting unready for the night was usually a quick affair, but for some reason, I wanted to look nice. I put on my pajamas—black shorts and a pink tank top—and put my hair up into a ponytail. Removing my makeup was fast, but I kept checking my face in the mirror. Was it presentable? I'd never not worn basic makeup around him before.

I laughed at the self-esteem issues I was fighting against; I was going to sleep here, and it certainly wouldn't be while having foundation or concealer. Still, my eyes had dark circles at the bottom as though I hadn't slept in a while—which I hadn't—and my face had some wrinkles I'd never noticed before.

After splashing some water on my face, I stared back at myself. "Get a grip," I muttered.

The floor was nice and cool beneath my feet as I stepped out of the washroom. Jack busied himself, stirring something inside a cooking pot. He'd changed into gray sweatpants with a white t-shirt, giving him an almost innocent look. I nearly burst into giggles at the thought.

He did a double take on me, his eyes lingering from my bare legs to my braless top. Food seemed to leave his mind as his grip on the spoon tightened, his knuckles turning white. I approached the island counter, and took a seat at one of the many stools, leaning forward. Knowing my breasts were pushed together at this angle didn't bother me, and it certainly didn't seem to upset him either.

"Is it too hot in here?" he asked in a gruff voice as he rinsed off the spoon he'd been using.

"It's just right." I stared around the place, letting my legs swing back and forth from the height of my seat. "Why?" I asked in an exaggerated innocent tone.

He snorted, but grabbed the cooking pot, and put it on a trivet on the counter. He grabbed some bowls, and served us some of the stew. The steam rose, and the smell was heavenly. My mouth watered, and I plunged my spoon in without waiting a single second. I ate, closing my eyes as I let out a moan. The meat was so tender and tasty.

"This is so good," I said, smiling ear to ear.

He simply watched me for a few seconds before eating his own food. We ate in silence for the rest of the time, the occasional clinking of dishes resonating in the vast room.

"You asked me a lot of questions tonight," he said playfully. "Does that mean I get an ask?"

I put down my spoon as my hand shook a bit; the last ask he'd had was when he'd fucked me. Was that what he'd ask again? How would I keep things professional if he kept doing things like this?

"It's a condition of our agreement, so I guess so." I made it sound so clinical.

He opened a drawer and took out handcuffs, a smile curling his lips as my eyes widened. "I'm feeling some... violent urges."

I swallowed hard; what did he want to do? Was he going to cuff me to something and beat me? Questions flew through my mind faster than I could keep up.

"Jill," he whispered my name, pulling me from my endless cycle.

I looked into his eyes. "What... What's your ask?"

"I want to lay you over my knees and spank you until my arm gets tired," he said in a calm tone; yet there was nothing calm about his gaze. If anything, it almost looked like his irises were darker than usual. As though he was already doing exactly what he wanted to me in his mind.

Whatever I was expecting, it wasn't that. It wasn't overtly sexual, but it wasn't the kind of ethical relationship I was trying to reestablish. Had it ever been?

"Why?" I couldn't help ask. "Why do you keep initiating intimacy with me, of all people?"

He arched an eyebrow. "You of all people?" He cupped my face, tracing his thumb along my cheekbone. "What do you mean?"

"You said you pay for sex when you want it, but if you wanted to... I don't know, spank someone for free, why not one of the women who flirted with you tonight? Most of them were tens like you. I'm..." I pulled away from him and stared down at myself for a second. "I'm just me." I didn't know why my sexuality was suddenly an issue, but he was on a level I could never reach.

Without warning, he threw me over his shoulder, and I screamed. I kicked and pounded against his back, shouting at him to put my down. What if I weighed too much? He'd pull a muscle and not be able to go into work.

"Now I'm angry..." he said through gritted teeth. "If you thought I'd be violent before, you're about to regret those words."

I protested as he put me down, spinning me around in one quick motion. My hands were cuffed before I knew what was happening. He sat on the edge of his bed and pushed me onto his knee. The other leg went over my legs, pinning me completely still. I'd never been restrained before and although my shorts were getting wet with arousal, I was scared. He sounded furious.

He tugged down on my shorts until my ass was bare, and I squirmed. "Wait. Why are you pissed off? What did I do wrong?" I asked in a higher pitched voice than usual.

His hand came down against my cheeks and I yelped at the shock. Again and again. I writhed, trying to get free but he only slapped me harder. Tears rolled down my cheeks as I cried out, my skin burning.

Before I knew it, he pushed his fingers inside my opening, and I panted heavily. I was soaking wet, and as he thrust in and out, my breath grew labored. An incredible climax clenched against his fingers, a harsh moan escaping my mouth as I came.

He unlocked the cuffs, gently massaging my arms as circulation returned. I sobbed in fits, unable to breathe properly. It wasn't the aching in my ass, but the tenderness he was suddenly showing me. He straightened me, then sat me on his knees, making sure my cheeks hung out as much as possible so he could keep kneading them.

"Deep breaths, darling girl. I've got you," he whispered in my ear. "But if I ever hear you putting yourself down about your amazing body again, I won't be as kind."

I laughed through my tears. "*That* was kind?"

"My arm isn't even a little bit tired," he said in a dark tone.

I knew then and there he could've gone on for much longer. Just the thought made my ass ache even more. "Understood," I said in a shuddering breath as he held me closer.

"When you're ready, feel free to go write your notes before you get to bed."

"Am I sleeping on the sofa?" I asked quietly.

He chuckled. "I think you already know the answer to that."

19

BITE

"What was your adolescence like?" I asked as I wrote in my notebook.

Sunlight beamed through the large windows, and I shifted my position so it wasn't glaring against the paper.

Jack smiled. "As any others, I suppose. I had my rebellious years, of course, but nothing out of this world. I was actually a pretty good kid, good grades."

"Friends?"

"A few, but by then, I was already a bit of a loner. I believe the word introverted was used by one of my teachers."

I scribbled that down. "We're you...hurting anyone at that point?"

"No." The word was simple, yet I could hear so many unsaid things behind it. He didn't want to tell me when he started killing. I could sense it.

"Have you ever hurt animals?"

"Also, no. Animals are always innocent. I never saw the point in harming any." He crossed his arms over his chest, averting his gaze. His jaw clenched, the muscle at his throat throbbing slightly.

A realization dawned on me, and I straightened. "Were you ever bullied?"

"I want to put forth a second condition," he said so suddenly as though completely oblivious to my previous question. When I arched an eyebrow, he continued, "I get one question I can skip until a time I want to answer it."

"Okay, but I get the same condition when it comes to an ask from you," I said, narrowing my eyes at him as my butt continued throbbing. Falling asleep had been difficult for multiple reasons, my aching ass being one. Him sleeping next to me was certainly another. Especially since he slept in nothing but boxer briefs.

"Fair," he said with a curt nod. "What other question do you have for me, then?"

"Are your parents still alive?" I asked, hoping this wasn't another delicate subject.

"My father died of a heart attack when I was twenty-three, and my mother passed away from cancer when I was thirty-nine."

I wanted to wrap my arms around him and hold him close. "I'm sorry." And I meant it; I knew what it was like to lose loved ones. More than once. That was part of that curse I was convinced I had.

"I think that's enough for today," he said as he got to his feet. I'd been interviewing him since we'd woken up, not even giving him a pause during breakfast. With everything I'd gotten, my report would be perfect.

"Mind if I take a quick shower?" I'd been looking forward to trying out all the different sprays.

"Of course. Towels are in the cupboard in the washroom. Help yourself."

I nearly ran through the door, too excited to try it out.

It was so big and had so many different jets; I could dance in here if I wanted to. Hell, a single mattress would fit in there. Part of me didn't want to lock the door—an invitation for Jack to come in if he wanted to—but I decided to follow the ethical path. My research methodology professor would die from shock if I told her what I'd done so far. Even the condition of an exchange wasn't great.

Well, some people gave away Tim Horton gift cards, and I gave away favors. Or *asks*, as Jack called them.

The shower was just as blissful as I imagined. I didn't want to run his electricity bill down the drain, so I still washed up as quickly as possible, enjoying every second.

When I was cleaned, I slipped on a summer dress, liking how it flowed from my waist to above my knees. Like a beautiful purple flower.

I stepped out of the washroom, hair still wet, but the towel had done a good enough job.

"By the way, thanks so much for all your answers before," I called out, assuming he was by his bed.

He came out of where there was a partition near the kitchen and grinned. "You'll still have plenty more notes soon enough after we're done today."

"Oh?" I approached.

He stood at the end of a large table, hands clasped behind his back as he stared at me mischievously. A small chocolate fountain was in front of him, along with dozens of strawberries carefully placed on a plate.

I approached, arching an eyebrow in silent questioning. Just as I was about to sit on the chair to his side, he grasped my wrist, holding my back.

"Oh, no no." His hand reached for the back of my dress, and my breath hitched. "My next ask has everything to do with the victim you said you wanted to see."

I trembled as his fingers clasped the zipper, and he

slowly began unzipping my dress. "No need to be so scared. You're not the victim this time." He continued until my dress was fully opened at the back. He gave my dress a small tug, and it fell to the floor.

Without warning, he picked me up effortlessly and laid me on the table. My whole body warmed at the thought of what I looked like.

His gaze raked along my body, inch by inch. I trembled as he seemed to look right into my soul. To dance with the one who offered my pleasure beyond anything else. Offered me to just let go of everything.

When he cupped my cheek, a tingling sensation shot across my skin. Rope came into view as he grabbed it off the side, and he slid it along my wrists, tying them together. A small gasp escaped my lips as he pushed my arms above my head and tied the other end of the rope to one of the table legs. His mouth brushed against my skin as he moved back slowly, taking his time with small kisses and occasional nips.

He tied another piece of rope to my ankle, then tied that to another part of the table, leaving my right leg free to move.

He leaned toward me. "I'm going to eat you alive."

Heat engulfed me at his words, and I instinctively pushed my free leg against the other, squeezing my thighs to stop the intense throbbing between my legs. It didn't help at all.

He grabbed one of the strawberries from the plate and slid it across my mouth. "Open up and keep it halfway in your mouth. Every single bite mark will be counted after I'm done..." He left the rest unspoken, but I had the feeling the punishment might be delicious.

The fruit was bigger than what I was used to—almost

the size of a small apple—but I did my best to hold it in place with my lips and tongue.

He grabbed another one of the berries, and this one, he dipped into the flowing chocolate before holding it over one of my breasts. My eyes widened just as the warm liquid dripped from the fruit and landed perfectly on my nipple. The sudden heat caused me to jump, and I whimpered as strawberry juice leaked into my mouth.

He chuckled. "That's bite number one." He kneaded my breast, hovering just above it as his gaze burned into me. "How many more can I get you to make, I wonder?" He licked my chocolate-covered nipple.

My pulse throbbed in several places, and I squirmed against the restraints. I needed him to touch me more. Needed to touch him in return.

He suckled gently on my hard tip while his free hand busied itself with my other breast. He fondled and squeezed, and a few more times, he managed to get me to bite down a little more on the fruit. Tears filled my vision as he brought me to the edge of insanity, and I wasn't sure I wanted to beg him to stop or continue. It was all so much.

Lowering himself, he trailed more kisses along my abdomen, then to the top of my thigh. "Spread your leg to the side for me," he hissed, and I instantly obeyed, my mind almost empty save for his voice and the pleasure flowing through me. I didn't need to think; my body trusted him beyond anything else.

For a second, he seemed almost surprised at my obedience as our eyes met. A hungry smile curled his lips. "You're being such a good girl," he said in a low growl. "Do you think that'll help you when I check the strawberry in your mouth?" He kissed my inner thigh, his beard tickling my skin, then muttered, "Because it won't. I'm going to take what's mine. And you'll take your punishment, won't you?"

When I didn't answer, he parted my labia and gently flicked his tongue along my center. I bit down harder at the same time as I moaned. At this point, the fruit was barely hanging on.

He delved his tongue inside my opening, and I arched my back, the restraints tugging against my wrists and ankles. My breathing came faster, and soon, dark spots filled my vision as he fucked me with his mouth. He captured my clit between his lips, and I bucked, moving my head side to side, crying out as the strawberry fell from my mouth and rolled to the floor.

"Ah, Jack... Please... I'm..."

He sucked harder, swirling his tongue around my sensitive nub over and over until a profound shudder released, and I came.

He lapped at my wetness, and I blinked a few times, my mind fuzzy with the post-orgasm high. His finger slid inside my wet opening, and I shook at the sudden penetration. "You're so very wet." He slid a second finger and curled them so they hit a spot that had my toes curling. "Don't worry. I'm not done with you." He glanced at the strawberry on the floor, then gave me a dark look.

I swallowed hard.

20

PLANNING

"*L*et's see," Jack said, holding up what was left of the strawberry. "I'd say that's about eight bites... What do you think?"

I stared at the fruit as though it was my worst enemy but nodded. He'd untied me and even let me go wash up real quick with a washcloth, but I still throbbed with need, wanting him inside me.

Not that I'd admit it out loud.

He threw away the strawberry in the trash as he walked toward the elevator, then beckoned me forward, motioning his fingers. I followed, unsure what he'd do next, but I wasn't about to question him, or it would make me look worried. Which I definitely wasn't.

We took the elevator down, and once in the basement, I swallowed hard. A chair sat in the middle of the room, facing toward the bathtub. I recognized it as the one that used to be in the bare room. What was it doing out here?

He gave me a little push toward it, and I trudged to it. If I sat, whatever he planned next would happen, and I wasn't sure I was ready for it. I took a seat and stiffened as he placed his hands against my shoulders. "Don't move from this spot, or you won't be writing any more notes for the rest of the next few days. Is that clear?"

I swallowed hard. "Yes." Did he mean that in the sense he'd break my hand or fingers? Or maybe just that he'd throw me into the room and leave me there to rot for a while? I didn't want to find out which.

He grabbed the black mask from the shelves, slipping it over his head so the black material around covered even his hair. My heart quickened at seeing him wear it again; it felt like so long ago when this was the only way I knew him. He opened the door to the room, but from this angle, I couldn't see inside, and I had the feeling he did that on purpose.

"Eight bites, correct?" he asked in his muffled voice, glancing over his shoulder at me as he slipped on his leather gloves.

I nodded slowly, unsure where he was going with all this. The door closed with a snap, and I waited, pulse throbbing in my ears. A scream echoed from the room, and I clutched the side of the chair. The man's words were muffled, but I caught a few.

Please. No. Mercy.

I dug my feet into the cement floor, stopping myself from running to the victim's help. Reminded myself I'd asked for this. There was the occasional whoosh of air and something landing in a soft crunch. I didn't want to imagine any of it.

The door opened again, and I tightened my grip on the edge of the chair, trying to stop from trembling head to toe. Jack pulled out a tarp with a man lying on it, then let it drop hard. The man's head hit the floor with a loud thud, and I recoiled, staring. His blue t-shirt had turned a dark crimson, the cut along his throat still bleeding out onto the plastic beneath.

"Eight stabs for eight bites." Jack motioned to the body with his bloodied knife. "Guess which card he picked."

I stared from Jack to the lifeless body; I wanted to get closer to see if there were any choke marks around his neck, but even up close, it wouldn't make a difference. That area was too bloody to tell without washing it.

"Jack of hearts."

He cocked his head. "Why not the Jester?"

"You likely use other methods than the normal four when they don't pick. That's their punishment." I stared into the eyeless black holes. "Isn't it?"

"Always so clever." He approached her. "No questions, then?"

I shook my head and wrote a few notes about everything I'd just witnessed. "Why didn't you let me be in the room while you killed him?" I asked, jotting down a few more keywords before looking back up at him.

"Because seeing someone take a human life while you stand idly by changes a person forever."

I know.

He pointed the knife at me, a drop of blood rolling from the blade and staining the paper. I narrowed my eyes on him. "You're dripping on my notes."

For a few seconds, he didn't move or speak. It was as though time had frozen, and even I didn't dare move. He was unpredictable, and although he played along being the interviewee, I had to remember what he really was. What he was showing me he was.

He laughed, pulling off the mask. The warmth in his gaze was a stark contrast to the cruelty that occurred. Something in the way he looked at me sent butterflies fluttering in my stomach. I smiled as he pulled away the weapon, and I went back to writing my notes. Everything I'd just witnessed.

"Do you dismember the bodies before putting them in the tub?" I asked, going back and adding a side note to the side about him not wanting me to see the murder.

"Depends on the size of the victim, but with him, he'll fit as is when I squeeze him in there," he said as he stepped over his body.

I giggled, and when he arched an eyebrow, I just waved my hand dismissively. "I was just thinking about you deciding to cut them up into little pieces depending on whether they can become pretzel-shaped." I cleared my throat and quickly averted my gaze. "Sorry." It was stupid to apologize, considering he'd done the killing, but making light of it also felt a bit wrong. Not to the deceased, but as though I was mocking Jack.

Again, he just stared at me in silence; I could almost see the wheels turning in the back of his mind. I didn't want to know what he thought. That was a dangerous game. Even though it would make for a great addition to my report.

He walked toward me, then motioned for me to follow him. I got to my feet, and to my surprise, my legs trembled slightly. Had this upset me? I didn't think it would, considering it wasn't the first time...

"Go back upstairs. Lye isn't something you should breathe in, so I'll do the disposing on my own."

I grabbed his arm, scared he'd suddenly go back without me telling him to be careful. "Isn't it dangerous for you too?"

He closed the gap between us and kissed the top of my head. It was so gentle and loving, I nearly burst into tears. "I have protective gear to keep me safe. Go back up. Finish your notes, and I'll be up a bit later." He gave me a tiny push into the elevator, then turned the key, sending it back up.

I pressed my notebook against my chest as I walked out into the main area, my thoughts floating elsewhere. All the little things he'd done for me flashed back into my mind, and I couldn't help but smile. The ice cream he'd bought me... staying awake to make sure I was alright, the gentle kisses. I imagined us living together and doing these things every day. Maybe not the killing, but the rest. It was bliss. Writing my report and what came afterward had been planned for so long... Could I really change my mind?

Could I dare to hope?

I slumped down on the sofa, staring down at the little book. I'd collected evidence for so long, I couldn't remember what I had done before. Focused on my bachelor's degree, but it was on the path to my final plan. Everything had been. From the moment I saw Jack murder my foster parents when I was fifteen years old, it was all planned out. He'd rescued me from Hell without even knowing it, and in return, I'd tell the world why people like him were needed. The justice system didn't always work. Some fell through the cracks, and bad people were allowed to hurt others without consequences.

Tears rolled down my cheeks, and I wiped them away before they could fall. What if I could stay with Jack after the final report was finished? Maybe I could teach a journalism class at the university. Maybe...just maybe, I could live.

21
______

NEED

*S*oft sheets fluttered across my skin, and I moved involuntarily, following a sensual rhythm. It was as though I was reacting on instincts alone, moving with *him*.

Him?

I opened my eyes, and although the room was plunged into darkness, Jack was visible. A shadowed outline thrusting slowly into me. I let out a tiny whimper as I slid my arms around his neck.

"I need you," he growled as he pushed in deeper, his lips coming over mine in a kiss.

Our first kiss.

His beard was rough against my skin, and I loved it. Our tongues swirled around each other. I nipped at his lower lip, and he groaned. He slid his arms under my back, holding me close as he pushed his tongue into my mouth, fucking me in more ways than one. I wrapped my legs around his hips, meeting his every thrust in need. He moved torturously slow, but it was so good. His cock stretched me, and soon enough, ripples of ecstasy flooded through me.

In one quick movement, he kneeled back, keeping my legs on his thighs as he pumped in and out faster. I lifted my ass, and he slammed into me harder. Despite the darkness, his eyes were visible, his gaze raking along my body as though he was trying to memorize every inch of me. I raised myself on my elbows, sliding off my tank top so I was fully naked. Like him. Together like this.

He grabbed my arms, pulling me to him. I straddled him, legs wrapped around him as we rocked back and forth. He licked at my lips, not taking his eyes off me as we continued fucking... no. This was different. We were making love. I cupped his face, arching to him as he thrust faster, slamming into me balls deep.

"Jack," I moaned his name, and he kissed me harder.

He slid his hand between us and kneaded my breast. "Jill...you're perfect," he whispered, and my heart seemed to skip several beats. "So perfect for me."

Without warning, he flipped us both, so I was under him again. He pulled out, and just as I begged him for more, he flipped me onto my stomach. Pressure tingled along my stomach as the mattress dipped, and he leaned close to my ear.

"Cross your ankles for me."

I frowned, unsure why, but I did as he instructed, trusting him to know what I needed. To know what felt good. He spread my cheeks, and I panted against the pillow, goosebumps covering my skin. He pushed inside my wet opening again, sheathing himself in one thrust. With my legs crossed the way they were, his cock seemed to hit a different angle, and I cried out.

"Ah... Jack," I screamed, arching back.

He pumped harder, barely pulling out anymore and

just thrusting. His pelvis slammed against my ass, and I sucked in a sharp breath; it was still so sore from the day before. But that mixture of pain and pleasure brought me to the edge. I reached beneath me, rubbing at my clit as I convulsed around his cock.

He pumped in and out, then arched, crying out my name as he came inside me. Slumping down, he was careful not to put his full weight on me. His breathing was harsh and uneven as his lips tickled my ear. "My darling girl," he whispered as he brushed my hair aside and kissed my cheek.

Tears burned my eyes as he pulled out, rolling to his side and gathering me into his arms. He leaned against his elbow, tracing a tear along my face. "Why are you crying?"

I shook my head and buried my face into his chest. "I'm fine," I finally whispered. "It was...intense."

He grasped my hand and brought my fingers to his mouth to kiss them. "I was watching you sleep, and I just...needed you. More than my lungs need air. And it was more than just for pleasure. I wanted you in a way I've never craved anything else in my life before."

I blinked a few times, looking at him in silence. "What are...you saying?" I asked in a hushed voice.

"That, like it or not, you're *mine*."

That didn't sound too bad at all. "I like that."

His gaze searched me for a second before he smirked. "You say that now..."

"Plan on trying to change my mind?" I asked with a grin.

"Oh, you'll change it on your own eventually..." He actually sounded a bit sad, but the possession in his gaze never left.

I giggled as I traced a finger along his chest. "Wanna bet?" I grasped his cock, then lowered myself until I was at eye level with it. I brushed my lips against his shaft, and he let out a shallow breath. Knowing he was into the rougher stuff, I kneeled and clasped my hands behind my back, waiting. A growl resonated from him as he swung his legs off the bed and got to his feet.

"You want me to take control from you?" he asked in a deadly purr.

I approached the edge of the bed, then lay on my back, hanging my head over the mattress. Opening my mouth, I took a deep breath as I stared at his manhood; at this angle, it looked too big to properly fit. He grasped my wrists, pinning them on either side of my head, looming over me like the deadliest creature in the world.

His rigid shaft pushed past my lips, and he took deep, shuddering breaths as he pushed in. I gagged when his cock touched my uvula but swallowed against it, breathing in through my nose as best I could. Writhing against his grip, I struggled, but it just made him pump faster into my mouth. My pulse throbbed between my legs at his rough handling of me, tears running down the side of my face. I loved this. I'd fantasized about a man using me like this, and he was perfect.

He groaned in blissful agony, spilling himself down my throat as I swallowed every last drop of his cum. It was salty and reminded me of his scent but stronger. I closed my eyes, and when he pulled out, I smiled.

"Clean it," he ordered in a harsh tone.

I spun onto my abdomen and grasped his cock, licking and sucking it until only my saliva was left. He grasped my chin, gaze penetrating into my very soul. "Good girl."

22

BAD THINGS

*O*ctober brought a rainbow of warm colors to the tree leaves, and I couldn't be happier. The season was cooling, and I was back to wearing clothes I liked instead of dresses constantly. In this weather, my favorite was leggings with a long top. Simple, comfortable and, depending on the bottoms, could have a variety of different patterns and hues.

I flushed the toilet and washed my hands, enjoying the scent of the new soap I'd bought—jasmine. Once done, I stepped back out into my living area.

"Who's Martin?" Jack asked, his gaze burning into my core. He held up my cellphone open to the texting app, and my breath hitched.

Oh shit.

I grabbed it from him, trying my best to ignore his continued glare. If looks could kill... except he didn't need his looks. He *did* kill.

Martin: Haven't heard from you in a while. Everything ok? Want to hook up tonight?

I almost snorted; he was just horny and wanted some.

He didn't care if I was fine when I asked for a place to stay temporarily. It had been weeks since my last text. And the first thing he texts me is for a hookup? How did I ever have a crush on this asshole?

Putting the device back onto the coffee table, I shot Jack the iciest stare I could muster. "Is there a reason you're going through my phone?" I frowned. "Wait. How did you even get into it in the first place?"

"I've seen you input the PIN several times," he said with a shrug. "And I saw his name and wanted to know why a man was texting you."

"You had no right." I placed my hands on my hips, annoyed at his snooping. "I'm allowed to my privacy."

He got to his feet, and I took a step back at the way he smiled. "Then consider me looking into your phone my ask for today after you've finished asking me a bunch of personal questions."

Guilt bubbled to the surface, but I pushed down against it. No, it wasn't the same. He'd agreed to this. Under some amount of duress...but he still agreed. "Fine."

I just hoped he didn't look further into my texts with Martin since it mentioned the software I needed him to install on my laptop. The one keeping Jack from murdering me.

Would he still kill me after the time we've spent together? The questions gnawed at my heart, and I didn't like it one bit. He said I was stuck with him, but was that until he got tired of me and ended everything?

I grabbed my notebook from the coffee table and sat on the sofa. "Do you keep trophies?"

He seemed reluctant to answer, taking his time to sit down next to me, all the while saying nothing. He didn't even look at me.

"I do keep trophies, yes."

I perked up at that revelation, quickly jotting down the answer on the paper. "What kind? Can I see—"

"No." The word sliced through the air. "You can ask, but it's the one thing I refuse to give you any information about."

I wanted to protest; I wanted to see if I'd recognize anything from my foster parents. Needed to confirm I hadn't imagined the white knight with a black mask and leather gloves snuffing their evil lives.

"Is there... a reason you don't want to share?" I asked tentatively, not wanting to push him too far; he already looked mad.

"Yes, but I'm not giving you that information either," he said with a smile that didn't reach his eyes. "Next question."

I pouted for a second as I returned to my notebook, curiosity burning through me. Still, I pushed it away for the time being and focused on my next question. "How do you choose your victims?"

"It depends, but most of the time, they happen to fall into my lap, so to speak." He glanced at me with a twinkle in his eyes, and I pressed my lips together.

"Are you saying I'm a victim?" I wasn't sure why I wanted the answer to this question; maybe to know where I stood with him?

He turned to better face me and slid his hand along my thigh. It wasn't sexual, and I relaxed a bit. I enjoyed it when he was affectionate, not just wanting me sexually all the time. It was a nice change from what I was used to with other relationships I'd had.

"You're an exception to the rule in so many ways." He gave my knee a quick squeeze in reassurance, then straightened. "As for victims, I just happen to have a sixth sense or something. I find a person that interests me, and after stalking them for a while, I usually find out they're like me."

"Like you?" I repeated with a frown.

"Bad people who are better off dead."

At the thought of him dead, I cupped the side of his face, blinking back tears. I didn't know what to say, but I hoped my expression was enough to convey how much I cared about him. He turned his head, kissing my palm and sending goosebumps along my arms.

"So you murder people who do bad things?" I asked, not bothering to write in my notebook; it didn't seem so important at that moment.

"Yes, but that doesn't make me a good person, Jill," he said in a dark tone as though following my train of thought.

To me, it did make him the hero. My hero. What else was it called when someone rescued another from horrible conditions? But I wasn't going to tell him that. Not until the very end.

Maybe there didn't need to be an end? The little voice that had never been there before Jack—the voice for life—nagged at me to reconsider. The plan could change. It had to. Things were different.

We weren't a couple; this kind of relationship didn't have a proper title. All I knew was I belonged to him, and he was mine. That was what we were to each other. And it was more than enough.

"I have to work tonight," he said, glancing toward my phone. "It's likely pretty late."

I nodded, standing up with him. "Do you work tomorrow too?"

"For the next six days. One of my co-workers is sick, so I've taken his shifts."

I felt like such a child at that moment, wanting to

complain about him leaving for work. Why was I suddenly acting like a baby? This was ridiculous. "I get it. In this economy, stuff is expensive, so it never hurts to have extra income," I said with a forced smile.

"Plus, I enjoy having people owing me favors," he said with a smirk.

I laughed, knowing that all too well from him. Still, he wasn't even gone yet, and I missed him already. I was becoming one of those sappy romance girls.

"By the way, one of the nightclubs where I work is hosting a Halloween party I've been invited to. I'd like you to come with me," he said, sliding his hand to my lower back and bringing me closer to him.

I shouldn't have felt as giddy as I did. It wasn't as though it was a date or anything. He was working, and I'd be there to enjoy the festivities...with him. I nodded faster than intended, almost bouncing my head off my shoulders. "I'd like that very much."

He grinned. "Before I leave, I have an ask."

"Okay..." My heart hammered faster, wondering what he'd ask for today.

He pulled out his gloves, then motioned at the sofa as he slipped them on. "Sit and spread your legs for me."

I just stared at him for a few seconds, blinking. Still, I didn't argue or ask for more details as I sat, face heating up with each pulse. He kneeled in front of me, caressing my thighs as he tugged on my leggings.

"Off."

I swallowed hard and wiggled out of them with his help. If it was possible to die from combustion, I might've done it then and there. This was somehow more intimate than the last times, the way he stared at me hungrily.

He pushed my panties to the side and took his knife

out. My pulse throbbed in my ears, and my legs instinctively tried to close against his.

"I have someone on my victim list I'm planning to hunt down in the next few days, and I want your scent when I take their life," he said in a growl as he flipped the weapon so his gloved hand held onto the blade. Slowly and without losing eye contact, he pushed the handle into my tight opening, and I gasped. "I want to smell you when I kill him."

I gawked at him, my breathing turning shallow into small gasps as he pumped in a few more times. When he pulled it out, he licked the handle, closing his eyes as though he was experiencing bliss.

"Jack..." I whined his name, needing more.

He smirked before putting the weapon away, then sliding his fingers into me. I arched back against him, and several minutes later, I came. Hard.

"I adore when you cum for me, darling girl," he said in a harsh whisper. He kissed the tip of my nose, and I smiled as he headed toward the door.

I already missed him.

I went back to my notebook, transcribing them onto my laptop for safekeeping. Plus, it was where I was writing my report, so it was just easier. As I got back to the place where he wouldn't answer about trophies, I stopped. Why wouldn't he talk about those? Where did he keep them? Likely in his home somewhere.

A devious idea popped into my mind, and I did a quick internet search. Just to satisfy my curiosity. It wasn't as though I'd actually buy a wireless video camera and hide it in his place so I could spy on him. And even if I did, was that really as bad as drugging me, breaking into my apartment, kidnapping me, and threatening me? Of course not. Spying was a lesser crime in comparison.

Before I could change my mind, I clicked the purchase button and put it out of my mind. It would be fine. I just wanted to see if he was hiding any trophies, and if I could just get a quick glimpse of them, that'd be it. No harm if he never found out.

All I had to do was find a good time to install it at his place.

23

RELATIONSHIPS

The package arrived the next day, and my heart was hammering so hard against my chest, I thought for sure my ribs would break. The camera only required batteries, and connecting it to my phone was the easiest thing in the world. Once I was at Jack's place, all I needed to do was connect to his Wi-Fi—which I had the password for already—and find a good spot to hide it.

I checked the time; he'd be at work. My pulse sped as I checked my bank account and made sure I'd have enough money to cover a taxi all the way out to his place and back. I'd mentally noted the address and was just about ready to leave when I remembered something vital. I didn't have a key to get in. I muttered a few choice words as I paced my living area, trying to think.

He opened the garage door with an app on his phone, but at one point, it hadn't worked properly, so he'd gotten out of his car and pressed a button to the side. It was hidden under some vines. All I needed to do was get into the garage, and from there, apart from the basement, nothing else required keys from what I'd seen.

My stomach churned the whole drive there. I clutched at my messenger bag hard, the hard lump of the camera beneath my fingers. Making sure it was still there.

Forty-five dollars later, I stood in front of his home, the floodlight the only thing I had to illuminate me in the darkness of the night.

I wasn't going to waste any time, though, so I strode down the slope toward the garage door. The vines were skeletal, most having only a few red leaves left, but the button was still well hidden.

"Not unless you know where to look," I said in a sing-song voice as I pressed the button.

I winced at the loud scraping of metal as the door opened. Not that there was anyone around to hear; most places around her were businesses that were closed at this hour. But still, sneaking into a serial killer's home—Jack's home—was one hell of a risky move that could end very badly for me.

Only if I'm caught, which I won't be.

I snuck inside, heart pounding. The door leading to the main area wasn't locked, as predicted, and I smiled ear to ear. So far, so good. I rushed inside, then froze. What if he was here? He could've left work for whatever reason, and if I was caught here... I trembled, not wanting to imagine what he'd do. I didn't think he'd kill me—not for something like this; he'd consider it too light a consequence. No, he'd just hurt me a lot for it. At the thought, my body tingled, and I pressed my thighs together.

"Seriously?" I whispered to myself. My body really did have a mind of its own, but I couldn't argue I didn't enjoy pain. Not when it was Jack doing it.

I shook my head, trying to focus. I had a mission, and I needed it done sooner than later. Definitely before he returned home.

Stopping in front of a bookshelf, I turned my back to it and looked around. From this angle, I'd get most of the main area—apart from the bed—which would be perfect considering the camera could move up and down and side to side remotely. All I needed was to hide it well enough.

I grabbed one of the stools and carefully stood atop it, reaching the last shelf. A few plants decorated that section, and I grinned when I realized I was right about them being artificial. No way would he water them constantly from this height, no matter how tall he was. Which was perfect since it meant he wouldn't snoop around this area too much.

The stool wobbled a bit, and I clutched at the shelf, grimacing as a few of the items below toppled over.

"Shit..." I placed the camera, angling it already where I was pretty sure he was hiding something. A large black desk with a locked middle drawer. Every time I went near it, he'd tensed up and watched me more intently. It might not be the trophies, but it must be something.

I bent down, placing the trinkets that had fallen over back to their place or where I thought they went from the markings of dust surrounding them. It didn't take long before the stool was back in place, and I was all done. All that was left was connecting it to the Wi-Fi, and... Voila! With a few taps on my phone screen, it was done.

Turning on the camera, I checked to make sure no lights were visible, and I relaxed when there were none. I'd checked ahead of time, but with my luck, once it was connected to the internet, suddenly, there'd be one. I placed myself in front of the ominous desk of secrets and waved up at the camera while staring at the feed on my phone. Perfect. This had been so easy.

My stomach knotted again, and I shivered. Too easy. And even if I didn't get caught, I was spying. On Jack, of all people. The man I trusted more than I should. And cared for more than I should.

I pushed the thoughts from my mind. It was already done, and I wasn't about to change my mind after all this effort. Instead, I took off, making sure to properly close the garage door behind me and leaving everything as it was.

The taxi took longer to arrive than I cared for, but as soon as it left his lot, I relaxed in the backseat. Despite everything having gone perfectly, I kept replaying every-thing in my mind, trying to find a mistake I'd made. The only thing that kept me from going insane was repeating to myself that even if I had fucked up, it was too late anyway.

Back home, I was restless, checking the camera feed every few seconds. He wasn't even supposed to come home for the next four hours. I was being stupid. Instead, I texted him a quick message about perhaps revisiting the topic he didn't want to talk about last time. I needed to put it in his head to think about the trophies and hopefully look at them.

The knock at my door made me jump, and I gasped as my phone fell to the floor with a clang. I picked it up and ran to the door, half-expecting Jack to be standing there. Had he found out somehow?

I checked the peephole and rolled my eyes as I opened the door a bit. Martin stood there with a charming smile.

"Hey, good lookin'," he said with a wink.

I frowned. "What do you want?"

He dropped the act and motioned over my shoulder. "Look, can we talk?"

I stepped aside and let him in.

"So what do you want to talk about?" I asked, crossing my arms.

"I was getting worried. You weren't returning any of my texts anymore..."

"Maybe because the last time I texted you, asking for help, you shot me down without so much as an *are you okay?*" I didn't mean to sound so angry, but apparently, it was still a sensitive topic.

His eyebrows shot up. "It wasn't personal. I just said I couldn't, and then I went to sleep almost right after. It was late."

I scoffed. "Sure. And the next day, you couldn't pick up your phone to make sure I was even still alive?"

"You're being a bit dramatic, aren't you?" Sarcasm dripped in every word. "You're acting as though we're in some kind of relationship—"

"I thought we were. You know... friends?" I shook my head; how had I never realized until then just how one-sided this was. "That's where the fuck-*friend* bit comes in."

He raised his hands. "Okay, okay. I screwed up. I should've checked on you. But the longer I waited, the weirder it got, so I just—"

"Waited until you were horny enough to finally have a reason to check on me? Yeah, thanks."

"Don't act as though having sex isn't what you wanted out of this too. I was horny, so I contacted you just like you text me when you want some."

More like when I needed favors. "Well, there won't be any more texts from me. I'm with someone now, and—"

"Found someone who could do more things for you?" His smile had turned cold.

My hands curled into fists. "It isn't like that."

He took a few steps closer. "You look me in the eye and tell me this isn't another one of your transactional friend-ships, as you call them."

I opened and closed my mouth, wanting nothing better than to scream at him. Tell him to go to Hell. Instead, I opened the door and pointed at it. "Get the fuck out of my place. And never contact me again."

"Fine." He marched out, glancing over his shoulder. "Stupid fat cow," he muttered under his breath as he went down the corridor.

I slammed the door before the tears fell. I didn't care what he thought of me, but it still hurt. He'd been a friend for a long time, and to know this was how he'd really felt all those years... No wonder he always closed his eyes when we were intimate in any way; he couldn't stand to look at me. I locked the door, then trudged to my bed as I continued crying. I hated him.

His words repeated inside my mind; transactional friendship. Was that all I was to Jack, too? Someone he kept alive to keep his secrets from coming out? I asked questions, and he got something in return. We both bene-fited in our own way, but it was an exchange nonetheless. Is that all I'd ever be good for?

I sobbed into my pillow, exhaustion lulling me to sleep.

A beeping noise woke me up, and I squinted through one eye, trying to find the source of the noise. I grabbed my phone, staring as the security camera app popped onto the screen. My heart picked up speed as I tapped it, trying to make sense of what was happening. It didn't help that my eyes burned from crying myself to sleep.

Jack walked into frame, and I sat up, watching intently. I glanced at the time, noting he must've just gotten back from work, and there was a text notification at the top of my screen. I lowered it just enough to read and grinned when I read his reply to my earlier message.

Jack: Not a chance.

We'd see about that.

He opened the top drawer on the right and then the two bottom ones to the left. I frowned as I watched, but when he opened the middle one, I realized that's how it unlocked. Smart.

Whatever he pulled out wasn't very clear at the angle, so I moved the arrows, trying to get a better view. The zoom in function wasn't great, but it looked as though he'd taken out a red binder. I held my breath, watching as he flipped through it, but before I could adjust the angle, he put it away.

It didn't matter; I knew where it was. All I had to do was go back to his place tomorrow while he was working to check it out. I'd take a few photos of whatever the content was, excited at the prospect it might be notes. My cheek muscles hurt with how much I was smiling. Maybe it wasn't the trophies I was hoping for, but whatever that thing was, it was important enough to keep it hidden.

24

TRUST

Sneaking into Jack's home was getting expensive. Why did he have to live so far out from downtown?

Privacy to murder.

I went back into his home, using the same method as last time. Before checking the desk, I grabbed a stool, pulled it to the shelf, and climbed. I didn't want to take the chance he'd discover the camera, so I took it down, proud I'd gotten away with all this. What he didn't know wouldn't hurt him—I kept repeating that to myself. Still, I couldn't help the pang of guilt churning my stomach.

When the camera was back in my messenger bag, I strode to the desk, eager to finally see what the red binder held inside. I pulled out the drawers in the same order he had, and finally, the middle one. My pulse quickened when the binder came into view, and I grabbed it with trembling hands. I let out a breath as I grabbed the cover and opened it.

Empty save for a note.

I don't tolerate betrayal, Jill.

The words didn't make sense at first. It was as though I understood them, but they weren't registering inside my mind. I dropped the binder and took a step back as though it would suddenly attack me. He knew. How? I closed the drawer and rushed to the door, grabbing my bag as I went.

Locked.

It was as though my heart was stuck in my throat, and I couldn't breathe. Why was it suddenly locked? What happened? The doorknob turned, but it hit something with a heavy clunk. I ran to the windows, but my heart sank when I realized most didn't open; the few that did had bars at the bottom or were too small for me to get out of.

My breath was shallow as I stared around. Black spots obscured my vision, and I crouched on the floor, dropping my head low. I had to think. There had to be a way out. No way would I stay here and wait for him to come home.

He already knows.

No. He couldn't. I'd been so careful. Chills ran down my spine as I straightened and looked around. The elevator. Maybe the basement had a way out of here. I ran to it, shaking as I opened the freight door and stepped inside. My fingers trembled as I pressed the button to go down, and I held my breath. All I had to do was find a door. Or something. If worse came to worst, I could hide somewhere and try leaving when he got back and the door unlocked again.

Why was it locked? The question kept repeating in my head over and over again.

The elevator stopped, and the freight door was already opened. My mind went blank as I stared at Jack.

He stood in the middle of the room, near a tarp on the floor, arms crossed. His calm exterior didn't match the fire burning in his eyes, and I took a step back. I'd never seen him this angry before. Was this what he looked like beneath the mask when he was about to kill people?

"*Jill, Jill, Jill*," he cooed my name, and for once, it didn't send the usual butterflies in my stomach.

I backed away as he approached, raising my hands up as though that would somehow stop him. "Please no. No, no." Tears flooded my eyes, and I didn't care I was crying. I was terrified. Not of death but of dying then and there. It wasn't time yet.

I backed into the corner of the elevator, and he stopped a few feet away. He was beyond angry; he was furious. He didn't look it, but I could tell by the way he stared at me. This wasn't something bargaining could fix.

"Do you really think I'd keep any trophies here?" he asked quietly. "And don't you think I'd already have cameras installed here to keep people out?"

My heart hammered in my chest. "I—"

"Imagine my surprise last night when I got an alert that someone broke into my home." He slid his hand behind my head, grabbing a fistful of my hair. "I watched you install that little camera of yours, and all I had to do was play your little game." He wrenched back, and I hissed through my teeth at the pain.

"I'm sorry," I whispered.

"Not yet."

"Please tell me how to fix this. I'll do anything. Please, Jack."

He stared at me for a few seconds. "You want to *fix* it?"

"Yes," I nodded despite it pulling harder on my hair. "I want... I need you to forgive me."

He scoffed and released his grip as he took a step back. "Betrayal isn't something—"

I fell to my knees and crawled toward him. I wasn't afraid of dying. Not even if it was then and there, but to have him angry with me in my last moments? That I couldn't deal with.

"Please don't hate me," I said through tears, gripping his black slacks and holding on as though he might rip me away. "I'm so, so sorry. I wanted to know, but it was wrong of me. I was wrong to do that. Please...I'll do anything." I sobbed harder. Every relationship in my life flashed through my mind as Martin's words repeated. Everything was transactional. I was nothing but a favor.

He grasped my arms and picked me up from the floor. "You'd really do anything for me to forgive you?" His thumbs traced along my skin, and I shivered.

"Yes." I didn't hesitate. Whatever it was, I wanted to prove to him I could be trusted. That I'd never betray him ever again.

He kissed me, and I melted into him. Wasn't he angry? Why was he being affectionate? When he pulled away, I panted against his lips, my heartbeat fast.

"I forgive you," he said quietly. "But I still have an ask..."

"Really?" When he nodded, a half-laugh, half-cry left my mouth. I nodded. "Anything."

He slid his hands to my back. "I want to chain you to a post and whip you."

It should've sounded scary, but I trusted him to know what he was doing. His pleasure was mine, and it was all I wanted to do. He'd forgiven me, and I couldn't be more relieved.

"Okay," I whispered.

He took my hand and led me deeper into the room. Near the fire pit, a long wooden post stood floor to ceiling. An old, rusted hook was embedded at the top, and I stared at it warily. "What's that for?" I pointed at it.

"Sometimes, I hang people from here." He pushed my hair to the side and kissed the crook of my neck.

"Kinky," I said with a scoff.

He laughed as he grabbed a pair of handcuffs and a long chain from the shelf. It didn't take long to adjust the chain so it hung low enough off the hook. He attached the cuffs to the chain, letting them hang there before turning his attention back to me.

"Strip."

I swallowed hard and, with trembling hands, pulled off my top. It was cooler down here, and goosebumps prickled on my skin as I unclasped my bra. I dropped both to the floor, then pulled down my leggings and panties together and stepped out of them. Standing naked felt suddenly embarrassing. I covered my breasts with my forearms while crossing my thighs a bit.

He smirked. "You acting shy isn't going to help you get out of this."

"I'm not trying to," I shot back. Before I lost my nerve, I walked over to the wooden post and leaned forward against it, raising my arms above my head. He cuffed my wrists, forcing me to tiptoe slightly. Trailing kisses along my spine, he sent shivers all over my body as I stood there at his mercy. My breasts pushed on either side of the post, the texture rough against my skin.

"I plan on making this hurt," he whispered in my ear as he pushed my hair to the front. "I forgave your betrayal, but you should still be punished, right?"

My pulse shot south, and I let out a whimper. "Yes."

I turned my head as he walked back to the shelf and grabbed a whip. My eyes widened as I recognized the type; a cat-o'-nine-tails. Not for beginners. It had several braids ending in riding crop tips, which meant each blow would snap against my flesh.

He motioned a finger for me to turn back around, and I did as ordered, not wanting this punishment to be any worse than it already would be.

The first blow came, and I tensed at the cracking sound before it even landed. I screamed, pressing my forehead against the post, trying to catch my breath. My eyes watered with the second one, and I cried harder. I wouldn't beg for mercy, though; I knew this was necessary. For both of us.

Over and over, he swung, and I shrieked, my back stinging. My lungs burned as though I'd been running without stopping.

"Relax. Don't resist the pain," he said between blows. "Breathe and focus."

I stared at a small crack in the wood, repeating to myself why this was important. It was a show of trust on my side. Taking responsibility for having broken his. For him, it was making sure I never did something like this again.

Before I knew it, the sound of his belt took me away from my concentration, and I stiffened again. Was he going to use that next? His zipper came down, and he sheathed his cock inside me in one thrust. I moaned, standing a bit higher on my tiptoes as he pumped into me as though he'd turned into an animal. He pulled out, and I whimpered at the loss of fullness, but he didn't stop touching me. Reaching in front of me, he kneaded my breast while his other hand stroked his shaft until...

His cum sprayed all over my back, and I hissed through my teeth as it stung a bit.

He uncuffed me, and I nearly fell. He held me, hands beneath my arms so he could avoid touching my sore back. Gently, he put me on the floor and straightened.

"Are you ready for a bit more?"

Tears dripped onto the cement, but I nodded. Yes. I could do this. Despite the pain, my body trembled with need for him.

He walked away, and I frowned as he stood in the elevator. Where was he going? Was this my punishment? To stay sitting here on the cold floor while my back throbbed? He motioned for me to come to him, but just as I tried getting to my feet, he shook his head.

"Crawl to me."

I gawked at him, unsure what to do. It wasn't anything bad, but the humiliation of it bubbled inside my chest until I wanted to sob. Yet, the idea of going to him where he stood, waiting for me. I took a tentative step with my hand, then the other, and soon enough, my knees followed. They hurt a bit under the pressure and hardness, but I focused on getting to him. I kneeled in front of him and waited. I wasn't sure for what, but more than anything, I needed his touch.

He pressed the elevator button, and I stayed still as it lifted us to the main room. When the freight door was opened, he took my hands and helped me to my feet. I opened my mouth to say something—anything—but I couldn't seem to find the words. Didn't know what to ask or what I needed.

Jack knows. Trust him.

"Can you walk to the shower?" he asked in a hard voice. It was as though he was still angry, and my heart sank. Had it not been enough? Did he actually forgive me?

I nodded, and he led me to the washroom, standing close.

He turned on the tap, and water sprayed from the showerhead. I stared at it, unsure; I knew I had to wash up, but it looked as though it would hurt. Was this part of the punishment?

He stripped off his clothes, and I stared at him. His cock was soft, but everything else about him was hard. "Face the water, and let it run off your shoulder so it doesn't touch your back directly."

I did as he instructed and grimaced as the water cascaded down my back and stung a few places. I pictured my flesh torn and hanging off the bone but quickly pushed it out of my mind. It wouldn't be that bad, and it wasn't helping my emotions.

He grabbed the soap, and I relaxed as his hands slowly ran over my sensitive skin. It hurt here and there, but nothing too bad. His spanking had left more bruises than this likely would.

"Are you...still mad at me?" I asked in a shaky voice.

"I'm angry at myself," he said in a harsh whisper. He took a step closer, and kissed the top of my head. "I wanted to hurt you, but when I did... I just want to protect you right now."

I turned, staring into his brown eyes. My chest squeezed, and the same words kept repeating in my mind.

I love him.

Oh, no. This wasn't supposed to have happened.

25

CLOSER

With two research papers, October became too busy. Jack still came to stay at my place from time to time, but our schedules were opposites, which made it difficult to spend time together. Yet, every time we were together, sparks continued to fly. I was still interviewing him, but instead of opening up more, he seemed more reluctant than ever to answer. I'd thought growing closer would've had the opposite effect, and I wasn't sure why he was pulling back.

I tried pushing my worries aside as I got ready for the Halloween party tonight. It was finally time to let loose and have some fun; I couldn't wait. A thought crossed my mind, and I lifted my long dress. My face heated at what I was doing, but I reminded myself if he could play games, so could I.

Yeah, because teasing a serial killer can't possibly do any harm.

I scoffed as I pulled off my panties, then tossed them into my clothes hamper. With those gone and already no bra, the only thing covering me was my vampire dress, and the thought sent excitement burning through me. Playing with fire was fun.

I'd never gone to this nightclub before, but it was easy enough to find; all I had to do was follow the people dressed in costumes. This place didn't have a line-up outside, and instead, the bouncers were inside for the night. I went in and was immediately assaulted with the loudest music I'd ever heard. The live band definitely explained it, but did the bass have to be at maximum? The speakers were shaking so much, I was sure they'd blow.

I pushed past people and grinned at some of the costumes; one man was dressed as a baby and was having a tantrum on the floor. Interesting choice. Mine wasn't anything original, though. Just a vampire. With my long, straight black hair, I matched the all-black dress and thigh-high socks. I gave my coat at the designated spot and put my ticket into my small purse, clutching it close to my chest.

Someone in full tactical gear approached, and my heart skipped several beats as I met with the familiar brown eyes peeking through the eyeholes of a full helmet. He leaned close, sliding his hand along my lower back. "Hello, darling girl. Come to suck my blood?"

I giggled, pulling him in a hug. "I don't know about blood, but sucking on something? Yes."

A growl vibrated through his chest. "You know, I have access to the employee's room. Don't make me drag you in there this early."

He took my hand, and I squeezed; it was so natural being with him, I'd often forget why we were spending this much time together in the first place. It was only for the interview, after all. Right? My chest squeezed at the thought.

He helped me onto a stool at the bar and then took a

seat next to me. "I ordered some nachos," he said over the music, and I smiled.

"Thanks!"

Another man sat on the stool next to me, and Jack's eyes narrowed. Without a word, he grabbed my seat and dragged it closer to him. It didn't seem to take any effort on his part, and though he didn't speak, the message was clear. And just when I'd been thinking this was just for our interview.

I was being obtuse at this point. Why couldn't I admit he might have feelings for me too? I knew why. Fear of losing him. I was cursed to have people die because of me, and I was terrified that included Jack.

Needing to distract myself, I slid my hand along the side of my leg. Higher and higher, just above my hip, so it was clear I wasn't wearing anything beneath. Without a word, I took a nacho, pretending as though I hadn't done anything out of the ordinary.

He leaned closer, hunger dancing behind his gaze. "Give me one good reason I shouldn't set you on the bar in front of me and eat you out right now." His voice was husky, and I shivered at his words.

"Because it's impolite to eat outside food in an establishment," I said with a shrug, waving my hand.

He grasped it, and I turned toward him, swallowing hard. "Are you taunting me with a game?"

"What game would that be?" I curled my fingers over his hand, tracing my thumb along his gloved knuckles. "I suppose if it was a contest for who has the fewer clothes, I'd win."

He growled. "You'd also win for currently having the most patience because I'm much too tempted to take you to the washroom and sheathe my cock inside you."

My breath hitched as his hand slid along my thigh, and

I opened my legs. I panted in anticipation. His finger brushed against the top of my mound, and I let out a shuddering gasp.

"Tell me to stop, or I'll take this a step further."

I nipped at his bottom lip and let out a soft laugh. "I dare you."

He grabbed my arm and pulled me across the dancefloor and into an employee-only room. He pushed me into a closet filled with cleaning products and locked the door behind us. My chest rose and fell quickly as I stared at him.

"Teasing me was such a bad idea, but daring me?" He took off his helmet and put it on one of the shelves. "I'll make you regret it."

I smiled. "Don't count on it."

He thrust his tongue between my lips, his hand sliding to my neck. Holding his jacket, I pulled him closer, lifting my leg onto a barrel as his fingers slid against my clit. My moans were muffled by him ravaging my mouth, taking what he needed and swallowing my cries as he moved faster.

I arched against his hand, rubbing myself harder as I edged close to an abyss of pleasure I needed so desperately. He found the perfect rhythm that sent a pooling heat from my core to the rest of my body. I moaned in his mouth as his thumb circled my clit. Tightening his grip on my neck, he swirled his tongue around mine as he rubbed against my sensitive nub, and I exploded in ecstasy. Tears ran down the corner of my eyes as I rode the wave of my orgasm, my cries barely audible as he licked at my lips.

He pulled away, his smirk sending a chill down my spine. But I wanted him still. Needed to get him off. I kneeled, and he helped me down. The floor was icy beneath my skin, but I ignored it as I undid his belt. It hung to the side, the clanking sound suddenly loud in our little nook.

His erection sprung out, and I licked the head, cleaning the pre-cum. He let out a shallow breath, and I smiled right before taking him into my mouth. He was always somehow bigger than I remembered, and I loved it. The tip pushed down my throat, and I swallowed against it as a guttural cry left his lips; I adored undoing him more than I wanted to admit. Knowing it made him feel good drove me crazy in the best way.

I grasped the base of his shaft, moving my hand up and down in the same motion as my mouth. I bobbed my head, suckling as I swirled my tongue around his erection. His taste was strong—like him—reminding me of every time I'd tasted him. I flattened my tongue, sliding it hard against the underside of his cock, and he grabbed at the back of my head. I looked up at him, meeting his gaze as darkness seemed to swirl behind his eyes. I swallowed hard, and his jaw clenched as he grasped a fistful of my hair.

"You feel so fucking good, Jill," he said in a harsh tone.

I pulled his cock out of my mouth, my hand still moving up and down as I smirked. "Language."

"Fuck," he nearly croaked and thrust his erection back into my mouth.

My eyes watered, but I continued staring at him through my blurred vision; all the while, he pumped down my throat without mercy. That's what I got for teasing him. But it was worth it to see him lose control.

He convulsed, pushing down my throat so deep, I thought the choker around my neck might break. I swallowed several times, desperate for air, but instead, his hot release poured down my throat. He pulled out, and I coughed, trying to breathe properly again.

As he pulled up his pants, I got to my feet, a bit wobbly

after the whole experience. That was mind-blowing. Before I could say anything about it, he pulled me in for a tight hug, and his lips brushed against my ear.

"Want to go back to my place and watch a horror movie?" he asked in a teasing voice.

Nothing had ever sounded so perfect.

26

A SECRET

"What do you mean for a month?" I asked as the lump in my throat tightened.

Jack bopped my nose with a grin. "The company is opening a new nightclub in Toronto, and I need to train the new bouncers."

I wanted to cry, pout, and beg him to stay, but I reminded myself I wasn't dependent on anyone. Not even Jack. Instead, I nodded. "I understand."

The horror movie seemed to have lost its appeal, but I decided then and there to enjoy the time I had with him before he left next week. I'd been alone for so long, I was more than capable of doing it again for a month. But why did it seem like such a long time?

"You can still send me basic questions by text while I'm away," he said, pulling me to him.

We were lying on his sofa, cuddling. I'd missed a good part of the story, too distracted by more important things as we chatted.

"So you can have a bunch of asks when you get back?" I said in a teasing voice.

He snickered but didn't deny it. That bastard knew what he was doing.

"Want to play a game?" he asked suddenly.

I perked up, arching my eyebrow. "What kind of game?" I asked wearily. The last time he'd surprised me with something, it involved murdering someone in his basement.

He got to his feet, and I followed suit, watching as he opened the top left drawer of his desk. I averted my gaze, still guilty about having spied on him to break into that piece of furniture. He'd forgiven me, but I hadn't quite gotten there yet. He placed something on the desk, and my pulse quickened as I stared at a metal butt plug. The flared base's jewel embedded inside shone in rainbow colors underneath the lights.

"You start at the other end of the room." He held up his hand. "You have five minutes to grab this while fighting me off. If you win, I'll put this inside you and take your pussy. If not..." His smile turned borderline evil. "I'll fuck your ass with my cock."

I opened and closed my mouth, but the excitement running through me seemed to have taken my words away. Instead, I giggled as I ran off to the other side of the main area, ready for the fight of my life. And I wouldn't be gentle. He was about to get hurt.

"I hope you're ready for a beating," I called out in a sing-song voice.

He approached the counter island and crossed his arms, waiting in silence. In full tactical gear, he looked menacing, but there was something missing.

I motioned at his head. "Aren't you forgetting one of the most important parts of your gear?"

He chuckled as he returned to the sofa to grab his helmet. Just as he slipped it on, I rushed forward but stopped in the kitchen. With the counter between us, I had somewhere safe to wait and hopefully get around.

"Cheater," he grumbled from beneath the helmet. His eyes were narrowed on me as though ready to pounce; I couldn't help my giddiness.

I didn't actually want to win this game. The thought of his cock in my ass sent my heart hammering against my chest; I wanted it bad. But the chase was thrilling, and I wanted to see if I had what it took to outsmart—and outrun—him.

He went almost completely still, with only his eyes following my every little movement. At that point, I knew I was fucked—literally—but made a run for it, anyway. I managed to get around the counter and near the sofa, but just as I approached, strong arms encircled me. I kicked up, trying to get free, but he just lifted me off the floor. Before I knew what was happening, he pushed me over the armrest of the sofa and lifted my dress up to my back. I gripped the cushion, pushing my face into it as I trembled in anticipation.

He slapped the back of my thigh, and I cried out in pain, not at all expecting the blow. And not there. My eyes watered, but I just tightened my hold against the soft material.

"If you move, the next one will be a lot harder," he warned in a dark tone.

I didn't dare. Not with the way my skin stung. I was willing to bet that one would leave a mark for a while. He moved away, and I stiffened, trying to control myself not to run off for more fun. I'd likely regret it—or my tender flesh would. By the time he got back, his buckle clinked together as though undone, and I held my breath.

"Breathe, darling girl," he cooed as the sound of his zipper being pulled down seemed to fill the room. "Relax."

Something cold and wet lathered between my cheeks, and I let out a shuddering breath as my rectum clenched. The tip of his member pressed against my tight opening, and I whimpered as he pushed into me.

"You can take me, Jill. All of me," he said between harsh breaths.

My fingertips dug into the cushion with each inch, and after what felt like no time, he slid into me deep. "Ah..." I let out a small gasp; I'd never had anal sex before, and the thought of him taking my last virginity sent butterflies in my stomach. Or maybe that was his cock pumping in and out.

A clenching sensation traveled along between my legs, and I reached between the sofa and my body to take care of that need. I slid my fingers over my clit, moving to the same rhythm as he was.

He leaned forward, and I cried out as he went balls deep inside my ass. "Want to know... a little secret?" he asked, panting against my ear.

I swallowed hard; he had the same tone as when I'd been caught with the camera inside his home. Before I could answer, he grabbed a fistful of my hair, holding me down. Not that I could go anywhere with him pinning me down.

"That little PIN of yours isn't real."

My whole body went cold, my eyes widening. "What..." He straightened, pulling out almost completely, then thrusting back in. "Oh!" My heart was going too fast; I couldn't calm down anymore.

"That boy toy of yours... He caved in so fast under pain," he spoke in a soft voice. "Admitted you...only needed something that looked...sophisticated." He pumped in and out faster, and another wave of climax filled me to my core. At the same time, terror mixed in with the pleasure, and I trembled violently. His cock pulsated inside me, and he let out a harsh grunt as he spilled himself inside of me.

As soon as he pulled out, I pushed away from him and took several steps back. Tears rolled down my cheeks as my legs shook beneath me, but I couldn't seem to stop backing away from him. He pulled off the helmet, and I could suddenly see the serial killer again. How long had he known? When had he gotten to Martin? Was he in his basement waiting to die, or had Jack already murdered him?

Jack approached me as he buckled his pants, and I raised my hands, trying to keep some distance between us. He didn't stop, though, and as soon as he reached me, I tried getting away. It was like fighting against a hard wall. One that gripped my chin and forced me to look at him.

"No more lies between us," he said quietly. "This doesn't change anything, except that you don't need to pretend to input that PIN every evening."

"It changes everything," I almost shouted, wrenching away from him. "That was the one thing keeping you from..." I didn't want to finish my sentence, but I had to. "From killing me."

"I love you, Jill." The words hit me, so I just blinked at him. "I don't want you dead." He pulled me closer, a gentle smile curling his lips.

I gripped his tactical jacket, tears still flowing down my cheeks. "I love you, too."

27

CURSED

I flipped through the channels, trying to find something to watch. But at this hour, there wasn't much in terms of programming. There was only a week left for Jack to come back, and I was growing restless.

Breaking news.

"Now what...?" I stopped on the channel as I watched on.

The woman on the television was speaking about a shooting, but it was the text beneath her that caught my attention. Toronto nightclub. My chest squeezed as I grabbed my cellphone and sent a quick text to Jack. I hoped everything was okay and if he could just let me know he was safe.

Minutes passed by as I glanced from the television to my phone. Still nothing.

People had been shot. A security guard was brought to the hospital in critical condition.

My stomach churned, and I tasted bile in the back of my mouth. I called the number this time. It just rang. It wouldn't stop ringing. Why wasn't he picking up?

I bolted to my feet, pacing the living area. What should I do? My finger hovered over David's contact; Jack had given it to me in an emergency. Did this count? He might've been working and just couldn't answer. That wasn't an emergency; that was a needy girlfriend.

Still, no one could blame me as I watched the news unfold. The same nightclub he worked at. No names released.

I tapped on David's name and waited. And waited.

Nothing. With a scream, I nearly threw my smartphone against the wall but instead tightened my grip on it.

My device buzzed, and I answered it without even checking the name. "Jack?" I shouted.

"It's David," his voice sounded strained. "Jack's been...shot."

The world around me vanished until I stood in nothingness. Everything around me was still there, but it stopped existing in those few seconds I stayed on the line. David continued about Jack being in the hospital. That he'd keep me posted, but I barely registered any of it.

"Jill?" David's voice brought me back. "Hey. It'll be alright. He'll be okay."

"Yeah... thanks." I dropped my phone onto my couch and walked a few steps before collapsing on the floor. My hands curled into fists, and I pounded against the wood, not caring if my downstairs neighbor complained. I didn't care. Not about anything. Why had this happened? I'd known I was cursed, but I still let him get close because I loved him. But if I'd really cared, I would've pushed him away.

I staggered to my feet and went straight for the drawer of my nightstand. Codeine. What was left of it. This pain could go away if I took some. Even if it was only for a few minutes, I just needed the anguish to stop. I needed to breathe.

What if David calls with an update, and you're passed out?

The little voice inside my mind was right, and I bit my lower lip. Instead, I took a chance and called Nina.

She answered on the fourth ring. "Jill? What's the matter?"

I burst into sobs, trying to get the words out about what happened to Jack, about needing to make it all stop. To stop the curse.

Shuffling sounded from the other side of the line. "Whoa, hold on sweetie. I'll be right there, okay? Stay on the line with me, please."

I nodded, trying to control my shuddering breaths, but nothing seemed to work. Why couldn't I breathe anymore? The room seemed to dim around me, but I shook my head. I needed to stay conscious. Needed to know Jack was okay.

Time stopped making sense as I waited to hear back from David and for Nina to arrive. This was all my fault; my parents and brother died in a car accident, my aunt died of cancer, and my foster parents were murdered. Ginette overdosed because of me. Everyone around me died.

Jack's not going to die.

My buzzer went off, and I yelped, running to it and answering. "Yes?"

"It's Nina." Her voice was gentle but strong, exactly what I needed in that moment. I let her in, and as soon as I opened the door to her, she rushed inside.

"Okay, you're okay," she said, bringing me in for a hug as I burst into tears again.

"I'm...sorry...I called...so late," I blathered.

"You did good to call me," she said, pulling me back before closing the door behind her. "Come. Let's get you sitting." She led me to the sofa, and I slumped down onto it, still clutching my smartphone.

"I haven't heard anything more from David yet..." I'd muted the television, but the words continued scrolling past the screen. My heart seemed to stop.

Security guard brought to hospital has passed away.

"No..." I refused to believe it. It was impossible. "No," I said louder as tears rolled down my cheeks. I hadn't told him... not everything. I had to tell him.

My phone buzzed, but I couldn't take my eyes off the television. Nina picked it up and spoke in a quiet tone as she got to her feet and moved away from me.

I wanted everything to end. I'd always prepared it, and this wasn't how or when I'd planned it. But fuck everything.

"Oh, that's good news," Nina's voice caught my attention, and I turned toward her, blinking. Hadn't she seen what was on the television screen? She pulled the phone away from her for a second and smiled. "The security guard who passed away wasn't Jack. There was a mix-up in all the commotion. He was shot, but it was a bullet graze. He's fine."

I shot up to my feet and nearly threw myself into Nina's arms. "He's alright!" I shouted, not caring if everyone in the building—hell, the street—heard me. Nina handed me the phone. "He's okay, David!"

"I'm so sorry for the confusion before—"

"No, no. I can't imagine anything makes much sense when you're being shot at..." I stopped and let out a breath. "Are you okay? I never even asked if—"

"I'm alright. Just a bit shaken up. Jack's getting stitches done, but he'll... well, speak of the devil. Hey! You can—"

There were muffled sounds on the other line. "Jill?"

"Jack," I burst into sobs again, unable to control

myself. He was alive. He was okay. I couldn't believe it, but I needed to. "I'm so... happy you're... alright."

"I am. Breathe in, darling girl. I'm here." There was a short pause. "I'm coming back early. I'm leaving on the first flight tomorrow, okay?"

David said something, but it was muffled. I just nodded, still smiling through the tears. He was coming back to me. Alive. It was the only word that repeated inside my mind over and over. Despite wanting to stay on the line with him until he got home, my eyelids drooped as though they weighed a ton, and Nina insisted I get some sleep.

"Get some rest now," Jack said over the phone. "I love you."

"I love you too."

Nina helped me into bed, and as she did, I opened my nightstand drawer and handed her my pill bottle. "I don't want these anymore."

Her eyebrows shot up, but she smiled as she took them from me. "I'm proud of you. You're so much stronger than you give yourself credit for."

I closed my eyes as my head touched the pillow. It should've felt better, but the nagging voice in my head kept haunting me.

He didn't die this time, but he will if he sticks around you.

"Get some sleep and call me after class tomorrow. We'll talk some more then, okay?" Nina said in a gentle tone. I knew she wanted to know more about Jack, but I wasn't about to tell her the whole story.

"Thanks again for coming, Nina," I said, peaking through one eyelid. "I appreciate you so much." Would she die, too?

Yes. Everyone around you dies.

I shut my eyes tighter, plagued by the memory of death surrounding me at every turn.

28

DEATH

My eyes stung as I clasped my warm mug of coffee. I was going to need more than one cup before I got to class. The heater clinked a few times, trying to keep up with this morning's frigid weather; at least it hadn't snowed yet. Not that it mattered. Nothing mattered anymore except the pain in my chest. I knew what I had to do to keep Jack safe, but it was easier said than done.

Like summoned by my thoughts, a knock resonated throughout my apartment. I slipped off the chair, but before I moved any more than that, the door unlocked, and Jack stepped inside.

I'd given him a copy of my keys so he wouldn't need to break in every time. I stared at him through my blurred vision, then dashed to him. Fuck pushing him away—I needed to make sure he was actually here. That he was alive. I wrapped my arms around his torso, hugging him as tight as he held me. His coat was still cold from outside, bringing me back to reality. To what I needed to do.

I took a step back and averted my gaze. "I'm...glad you're okay."

"Jill?" He grasped my chin, tilting my head back so I'd look at him. "What's wrong?"

I shook my head, pulling away from him. "I just... I need to focus on my final report from now on. You almost getting killed made it impossible for me to work. Besides, I...need to make sure I'm following the correct methodology of an interviewer-interviewee relationship. A professional one from now on." I tried not to throw up, the bile burning the back of my throat.

"You're obviously still upset about yesterday and aren't thinking clearly," he said quietly, but the ghost of a smile touched his lips as though he knew I was spouting bullshit. "Why don't you ask me some questions? It'll make you feel better."

"I have classes I need to get ready for." I rubbed my arms; his icy stare seemed to freeze me in place. "I...also don't have any more questions I need to ask."

He cocked his head. "Is that so? What about the one I'd withheld for another time? The one about whether I'd ever been bullied?"

I'd almost forgotten about that. "Were you?"

"Is that a question, then?" he asked with a smirk. When I frowned, he just chuckled. "Tell you what. Since you're getting ready for class, how about I come back tomorrow morning, and you can ask me then."

I swallowed against the lump in my throat and nodded. "Okay..." But I didn't want him to leave. I wanted to beg him to stay. That even if I didn't have any questions left for the interview, I had millions of questions I wanted to ask him so I could find out more about who he was. What his favorite color was. What season he liked best. But I was too scared. Too terrified he'd die because of me.

He pushed a strand of hair behind my ear. "What aren't you telling me?"

"You wouldn't understand." The words came out harsher than I'd planned, and I quickly grabbed his wrist to keep him from leaving. I was giving way too many mixed signals, but I couldn't think straight. "I... People die around me all the time. My parents and brother, my aunt, my fos..." I bit my lower lip. "My friend overdosed because of me. Even Trevor and Martin are dead now. And you got shot, and I thought you'd died too."

"Those last two were my doing, not yours. As for your family, they died in a car accident when you were an infant. Not sure how that could've been your fault." When I nodded, he continued, "And your aunt?"

"Cancer..."

"Last I checked, you're not cancer. And unless you forced pills down your friend's throat, that also wasn't your fault." He kissed the top of my head. "And I didn't die. I will someday. So will you and everyone else you've ever known, but that's because we're human. Death is part of life."

"But—"

"If you're trying to get rid of me, it's not going to be this easy," he said with a smile as he brought me in for a hug.

I cuddled against him, breathing in his familiar wood and musk scent. His words repeated in my mind; all these years, I was sure I'd been cursed, but maybe that wasn't the case at all. Death just happened, and it wasn't my fault. I didn't want to move, too comfortable in his arms. Why couldn't we stay like this forever?

"The last two died because of me, though..." I said quietly against his chest.

His chest vibrated as he laughed. "They touched you,

so they had to die. That's not your fault; that's because of my jealousy." He cupped the back of my head, his mouth brushing against my hair. "And if I find other men who touched you, they'll die too."

"You can't just kill everyone I've ever been with," I said with a grin; he was getting pretty close to accomplishing it.

He pulled me away, darkness dancing behind his gaze. "Don't bet on it." He leaned forward, closing the gap between us with a gentle kiss. Nothing sexual, just affectionate.

"I'm really happy you're alive," I whispered against his lips.

"So am I." He gave my ass a playful slap. "Now, get ready for class, and I'll be by tomorrow morning, alright?"

"Okay," I said as he opened the door.

He glanced over his shoulder. "And if this is, in fact, the last question you ask me, I'll make sure my final ask is memorable." He gave me a wink before leaving.

I stood in my living area, staring at my door as the locks turned. Footsteps echoed from outside, and I blinked a few times. His final ask... What would happen after I finished interviewing him? I still had to integrate the information I'd gathered into my report. The threat of the PIN was over... There was nothing stopping him from killing me at this point. No more threats looming over his head.

He loves me.

And I loved him, but I knew love might not be enough to spare me. He'd never left witnesses before...except once about twelve years ago when he left me behind. He hadn't known I'd been hiding in the washer-dryer closet, though. If he had, I'd probably be dead, along with my foster parents. Instead, he became my hero that night.

I finished drinking my coffee, nearly chugging it as I grabbed my messenger bag. My two classes were apart by around four hours, so I'd use that time to work on my report some more. I made sure my notebook was in my bag along with my laptop, and I dashed outside.

The weather was freezing in comparison to the inside of the building, the wind hitting me like shards of ice against my skin. Thankfully, it was only cold and hadn't snowed yet since that would've slowed me down a lot. But walking against the wind wasn't great.

By the time I got to my class, my face stung and throbbed, but at least I was inside again. Away from the windiest day I'd had the misfortune of traveling in. I promised myself I wouldn't complain about the summer heat after this but snorted at my own thought; I swore the same thing every year. I hated both extremes and just wanted someplace to have a perpetual spring and autumn instead. Was that so difficult to ask for?

The day seemed to crawl at a snail's pace. I couldn't stop thinking about Jack and what his last ask would be. The thought of never hearing him ask for that again made my heart ache. I hated myself for having grown so dependent on him. On needing him.

As my final class came to an end, I stretched long and hard. I hated this stupid schedule; having a class finish at ten o'clock at night was torture. I was a night owl, but with a class earlier in the day, it just screwed my whole sleeping routine.

Elsie leaned against my side of the table with a grin. "Want to come have drinks with me and the girls? We're heading out right after we stop at our dorms to get changed."

"I don't know..."

"Oh, come on. You never want to go out. All you do is work," she said with a teasing smile. "Once. Just once. Please?"

I wanted to refuse, but then I imagined sitting at home, thinking of Jack. Wondering what he'd ask for. Wondering what came next in our strange relationship. "Sounds good..."

Elsie nearly screamed in glee as she bounced on her feet while clapping her hands. "Awesome. Okay, we'll meet back at this building in around thirty minutes?"

"Sounds good," I said, part of me regretting agreeing to this. I could've also gone home to work some more on my report, but Elsie was right—all I did was work. That or watch some television to pass the time. And occasionally do some scrapbooking.

This could be an opportunity to have fun.

29

OWED

I slipped on my knee-high boots before glancing at myself in the closet mirror. My tights were opaque and matched well with the black and red dress I'd picked out. It had slits on both sides going up to my thighs, while the front had a half-circle cut out, revealing my chest. Nothing too sexy, but I wanted to fit in at whatever club we were heading to.

The frigid air cut through my clothes, and I tightened my coat; the wind was messing up my hair, but worst of all, it was biting every part of me. God, I hated winter.

A group of women stood huddled together near the entrance to the building where my class had just taken place, and I recognized Elsie right away. She waved her hand, bouncing up and down. I guessed it was partially to stay warm.

"You made it," she said with a huge smile. "Come on."

We quickly rushed inside, and I rubbed my hands together, trying to get feeling back into them. "You had to pick the windiest day?" I asked with a grin as I did my best to flatten my hair. They frizzed like crazy from being outside for only ten minutes.

"Hey! I don't control the weather," she said with a pout. "Besides, cold or not, I'm having fun tonight! It's almost the end of the semester, and I'm celebrating."

I couldn't believe how quickly December had arrived, but I wasn't complaining either. Soon enough, we'd go on break for the holidays, and then my last semester would start.

We walked toward whichever nightclub they'd decided on, keeping to the inside as much as possible. It was so much nicer indoors with the heaters going. Soon enough, my skin grew sticky with sweat, and I regretted keeping my winter coat on.

"We'll go out here," one of the women said. I think her name was Sabrina.

As we stepped back into the night air, my sweat turned icy against my skin, and I shivered loudly. This was bullshit. Why had I agreed to go out?

To have fun with friends for once in your life.

I pushed away the annoying thought and continued on, focusing on my feet and trying to keep my head low against the freezing wind. Each blast stung my face, and I gritted my teeth, desperate not to shatter into a million pieces.

I slowed my steps as I recognized the path we took. "Wait. Where are we going?"

"Dominion's," Elsie said loudly over the wind. "Ever been?"

My stomach churned at the thought of stepping foot in there after what happened last time. Being passed around to give blowjobs to Lee's friends as though I was nothing more than trash. Ginette dying next to me while I was passed out. I hadn't gone back since that night. Since the time I'd quit taking codeine.

"You guys know that's a shady place, right?" I said, my voice shaking a bit, but I just blamed it on the cold. I wasn't scared. Not really.

Sabrina shrugged. "It's fine. Besides, they've got the best deals in the city when it comes to drink prices."

"You're not going to suddenly bail, are you?" Elsie asked with a pout. "Come on. We haven't even started the night yet. You can't go."

I wanted to argue, beg to go someplace else, but the rest of the group continued on, leaving Elsie and me behind. I bit my lower lip but finally nodded. I didn't want to stay in the cold any longer than necessary. Besides, it would be fine to go in. I wasn't doing drugs anymore, nor would I ever start again.

We entered, and a shiver shot down my back. It looked the same as before, the same furnishing and placement. The same creepy stairs going down into the basement to the toilets. We went deeper into the establishment, techno music blasting on all the speakers as people danced in the middle of the main room. A few booths and tables stood to the sides where people sat and chatted—although most were making out since it was nearly impossible to hear one another in this place.

Elsie motioned to a table, and we all took our seats, slipping out of our coats. It was nice being warm again, but my skin prickled as it defrosted too quickly. I winced as my thighs throbbed from the cold, and I got back up.

"I'm just going to use the washroom," I said loudly over the music. They all nodded, barely paying attention to me as they talked about what drinks to order first.

I went down the steps, my hand against the wall as I trudged down; the place was too cheap to install a rail. The paint was chipped in a few places, and graffiti covered most of it. Most of the stalls had missing doors, but I stepped into one that was whole and pulled down my tights to use the toilet. My thighs were bright red, and I grimaced as I rubbed them, trying to get circulation back. I could've stayed where it was warm at home. Instead, I was here partying with people who had something to celebrate. Me... Well, I didn't see much point in celebrating the end of the semester when all it did was bring me closer to using the card Jack made me pick.

Would he do it if I asked him to?

I pushed the thought from my mind; it wasn't time yet. Still had my report to finish before it came to the end plan. I flushed the toilet using my foot—no way would I touch the handle with my hand. No soap, but at least they had a bottle of disinfectant. I made sure to use three pumps. This place was beyond gross.

As I went back upstairs into the main area, I looked around, trying to find someone from my group. None of them were at the table anymore, but there were so many people around, I couldn't see any of them. I pushed through the crowd, heading toward the bar, when someone grabbed my arm.

Lee grinned, staring at me from head to toe. "Well, well. Would you look at what the cat dragged in?"

I tried wrenching away from him, but his grip tightened.

"I don't want any trouble," I said, narrowing my eyes on him. How I'd ever done any sexual favors for this scum, I'd never understand. But drugs made me desperate.

"That's fine. Neither does my boss." He leaned closer, his blue eyes eerie in the flashing lights. "He wants to speak to you."

"What?" My heart beat a little faster as I tried pulling away again. "No."

His fingers dug into my arm, and I winced. "I'll drag you to him if I've got to. Maybe involve your friends, too?" He motioned to the dancefloor, where Elsie and Sabrina danced. Bile burned the back of my throat at the thought. Not only of having them involved but them finding out what I used to do and why.

"Okay, okay. I'll come with you. Just leave them out of this."

I didn't fight as he led me through the crowd toward the back, where we went through an employee's only door. We walked through multiple corridors, passing by staff that didn't even blink an eye at Lee, walking me as though I was a kid who got into trouble.

At the end of the hallway, a black door called out ominously, a bouncer standing in front. He reminded me of Jack, and suddenly, I got a little more scared of what could happen next. The man opened the door, letting us through without a word, and I stepped inside. The room was vast and open. A desk stood in the middle, and the man behind it looked like something out of a gangster movie. He was tattooed from the neck down from what was visible of his skin, his hair cut short as though he was in the military. His dark gaze focused on me as he beckoned forward.

I yanked free of Lee and marched to the desk, trying my best not to tremble at the sight of the half-dozen other men standing around. Some were sitting at tables doing god knows what, but all eyes were on me.

The boss gave me a cold smile. "Lee noticed you come in, and I just had to finally meet you face to face." He waved to me. "The famous Jill."

A few people chuckled as I curled my hands into fists. I

wanted to punch him in his smug face, but most of all, I didn't want to tremble in front of any of them. "Well, we've met. Can I go now?"

He ignored my comment as he got to his feet and put out his hand. "My name is Noah."

I hesitated for a second before shaking his hand, doing my best not to whimper at how hard he squeezed my fingers.

"Great to meet you. Can I go now?" I asked again, half-expecting him to laugh at my request.

"Of course," he said with a smile. I couldn't believe my luck, so I turned and strode toward the door where Lee still stood. "However," Noah called out, and I froze, "there's still your payment we need to talk about."

My pulse throbbed in my ears as I turned back to the boss. "Payment?" I asked as my stomach seemed to roll on itself.

"Well, yes. You see, Lee here was giving you discounts on..." He frowned as he glanced toward one of his men. "Codeine, was it?" When he nodded, Noah grinned. "Yes. Well, he didn't have permission to do that, so you owe an outstanding amount."

"Wait, what?" I nearly shouted the words. "No, no, hang on. I made deals with Lee each time. If he fucked you over, that's on him, not me."

The man by Noah's side smirked. "Oh, he paid his price for that."

I stared toward Noah, and he lifted his hand, showing his pinky finger was missing. That had to have happened after the last time I'd seen him. Shit.

"How...much do I owe?" I asked quietly, looking back at Noah.

"Five thousand."

"You've got to be kidding me!" This time, I yelled and

didn't care. I was getting more terrified by the second but also a lot angrier.

Noah's glare could've burned through me. "Interest. You didn't pay for over a year, so your amount increased."

"By what, fifty percent? I couldn't have owed more than like, what? Twenty dollars per pill?"

"He discounted it by fifty, actually." He looked over my shoulder. "He's lucky he only lost *one* finger for that."

"Well...can I get some sort of payment plan that doesn't involve cutting any of my appendages?" I asked, my voice sounding small to my own ears.

Noah straightened. "Of course. You can pay half now and half tomorrow."

"This may shock you, but I don't have twenty-five hundred on me right now." I crossed my arms over my chest, hoping to keep my fingers safe from the psychopath.

He smirked. "I didn't think you did. So, instead, you'll pay me the total amount tomorrow, and for tonight, you leave with a warning."

I wanted to ask if it was a verbal one, but before I opened my mouth, a foot connected with my back, and I fell to the floor. Breathing was impossible, even through tiny gasps. Another kick on my upper back sent fire throughout my body, and I cried out.

Jack. Help.

The man Noah had been speaking to grabbed a fistful of my hair and pulled me off the floor. I screamed, grabbing at his hand and trying to relieve some of the pressure on my scalp. Lee walked up to me and backhanded me across the face. My lip burned, and copper filled my mouth as I stared at the floor with a blurry vision. Was I crying?

He did it again but on the other side, and my ears rang.

"I'm going to make you pay for my finger," he said

through gritted teeth as his fist slammed into my abdomen, and I doubled over.

I took sharp breaths, tears and snot rolling down my face.

I fucked up coming back here.

30

BEATEN

I buried my head into my pillow as my whole body throbbed. There were no more tears; I'm pretty sure I'd cried all of them out last night. Lee made good on his threat and made me regret he'd lost that finger of his. My throat was raw from all the screaming, and I winced as I swallowed hard.

The beating was bad but still owing that much money was worse. I had access to that amount, but it was to pay my tuition fees. Without it, I'd have to either pick up way more hours as a teacher's assistant or get a second job. And even then, would I make the payment in time? It would be due at the start of January.

The sound of the door unlocking sent goosebumps across my skin, and I pulled the blanket up higher to cover my face. If Jack saw me... I didn't want to explain what had happened. Or why it had. I didn't even know what I looked like, but it couldn't be good with the way I felt. I was so ashamed of having gone there last night. I was such an idiot. Going back to that place...

Stupid! Stupid! Stupid!

"Good morning, sleepy head," Jack said cheerfully. The mattress dipped beneath him as he sat on the edge of my bed. "Are you alright?"

I wanted to cry, and scream that nothing was okay, and to just cuddle up to him. Instead, I did my best to clear my throat before speaking, "I went out with a bunch of girl-friends last night. Went to a club and... I drank too much. Hangover."

"Is that right?" I could hear his smile. "I suppose that means you're not in the mood for interviewing me?"

"Sorry... Could we postpone it just a bit please?" I let out a breath. "I'll let you know when I feel better and we can meet up at that point."

He stayed silent for a few seconds. "Why won't you look at me?" he asked in a quiet tone that sent a shiver down my spine. He knew something was wrong, but I didn't want to admit anything to him. I was so ashamed.

"I'm... I have a splitting headache, and I didn't take off my makeup last night, so my face is a mess. Please. Just go. I need to sleep before my head splits open." I wasn't entirely lying; I couldn't imagine what my pillow and blankets looked like since I hadn't removed my makeup when I'd gotten back last night.

"Alright. I'll let you get some rest," he said. The mattress straightened as he got to his feet. "Call me when you're feeling better."

"I will. Thanks." I wanted to reach out to him, beg him not to leave me alone with the memories of getting beaten. The pain had been... I thought I'd died a few times. That my ribs had punctured my lungs.

The door closed, and the sound of the locks seemed to resonate inside my tiny apartment. I laid there, too sore to move, but I knew I had to get up eventually. Take a shower. Assess the damage. How long would it take to heal? I'd have to avoid Jack until then.

I trudged to the washroom and stripped down naked. Bruises and cuts covered most of what I could see of myself in the mirror, including fingermarks on my arm where Lee had dragged me from the main club to the boss's room. I'd been such an idiot to go back there. And what happened to Elsie and the other women? Had they just assumed I'd ditched them and gone home without a word? My face was smudged with makeup and blood with my lip split at the bottom. No wonder it throbbed so much.

As gently as I could, I cleaned my face, wincing every few seconds as I moved the wrong way; it was as though my whole body had gone through a grinder. I was tempted to take a shower, but the thought of water hitting my sensitive skin sent shudders through me, and I decided against it. Instead, I just slipped on my bath robe and left the bathroom. I just needed some more sleep, and I'd be okay in no time.

I gasped when I locked eyes with Jack. His expression was unreadable as he approached me; but fury danced in his eyes. He raised his hand as though to touch me but froze as though unsure if it would hurt me or not.

"Do you need to go to the hospital?" he asked in a quiet tone. He cupped the back of my head, his gaze searching mine.

"No, they just...beat me up." I wanted to make sure he knew nothing else had happened; something I knew I was extremely lucky about. "I'll be fine."

He pulled me in for a gentle hug. "*They*," he repeated in a growl. "I want names, Jill."

"Please leave it alone," I whispered against his chest as tears flooded my eyes. I didn't want him doing anything that could get him killed or caught by the police. It wasn't that I didn't think those men deserved to die, but I just wasn't worth the trouble.

"Why did this happen?" he asked; there was no judgment in his tone, and so I was comfortable enough to explain the situation.

He remained quiet for a few minutes, just holding me against him; gently as though he was afraid of breaking me. "Let's get you to bed." He led me to the room separator and helped me under the sheets. I turned my pillow to the other side, disgusted with how filthy it had gotten from before. That's what I got for not washing my face until then.

"Do you have an ice pack?" he asked as he tucked me in.

"No, but I have some frozen veggies I could use."

He shook his head. "You'll want something that's easier to hold to your face. Tell you what... I'll go to the pharmacy and get you some supplies. How does that sound?"

"I can't ask you to buy me——"

"You are worth every dollar I'd be spending and more." When I opened my mouth to argue more, he raised his finger for silence. "I won't hear another word about it. I'll be right back."

He got to his feet, and I closed my eyes, letting myself sink into my mattress; it was suddenly the softest thing in the world. Like fluffy clouds. The front door closed with a click followed by the sounds of the locks, and my pulse slowed. I was alone again. I hadn't wanted Jack to see me like this, but he'd known something was wrong. I guess telling him I was too hungover to ask him questions was pretty suspicious on my part; I could've been on fire and wouldn't pass on the opportunity.

I reached out toward my nightstand, and frowned when I couldn't find my phone. My body ached with every little movement, but I turned to my side, trying to find where I'd put it, but it wasn't there.

"Where…" Had I left it somewhere else after I'd gotten back home last night? The trek was still fresh in my mind, limping in the freezing cold.

I got out of bed, my legs trembling beneath me as I trudged into the living area of my apartment. It was cool, and I shivered as I spotted my smartphone on my kitchen table. With a small shake of my head, I went to it, convinced I was losing my mind; this wasn't a place I usually put it. I must've really been out of it.

Something in the back of my mind rang with alarm bells, and I pressed the button to wake it up from sleep mode. After tapping in my PIN, my pulse sped at what was last on the screen. The device's map showing where my phone had last pinged. It showed the path I'd taken from the nightclub. My stomach churned as I stared toward the door; Jack had gone there to kill them. I had no doubt about that.

As quickly as my body could manage, I rushed to get changed since I'd be damned if I went out in nothing but a bath robe. Still, I wasn't dressing to impress as I slipped on a pair of sweatpants and an oversized hoodie. I had to stop him; I didn't want him getting caught. He might've had no issues with murdering one person at a time, but there were half a dozen men in there. Maybe more.

Please don't let it be too late.

31

THE PLAN

The nightclub was eerily quiet. I knew at this hour it would be, but there was something more that hung in the air. I recognized it like an old friend: death.

The employee-only door was ajar, and I stepped into the hallway, the smell of copper and smoke assaulting my nostrils. Bodies lay on the floor with bullet holes in their heads. One closer to the front had his throat sliced open, and I guessed he'd killed the first one as stealthily as possible before pulling out a gun.

It wasn't like him to use that kind of weapon. Stabbing, drowning, and hanging, yes. Shooting? No. There were muffled voices coming from the boss' room, and I slowly pushed the door open to peek inside; it was a massacre. At least five people were shot dead lying on the floor where I'd been beaten the night before. There was a strange kind of ironic poetry to it.

Noah kneeled in front of Jack as he pointed his pistol straight at his head, his black mask and leather gloves all too familiar to me then. For a split second, I was back inside the washer-dryer closet in my foster family's RV, watching as he dragged Melanie to the bathroom. I couldn't see him drowning her, but the struggle and splashing around was clear. When he was done, he returned to where my foster father, Don, was tied up. Jack put a rope around Don's neck and dragged him into the living room area. He'd tightened the rope as my stepfather turned blue, and all I could see was how my nightmare was finally coming to an end.

In that moment, I'd wanted to reveal myself and ask him to kill me, too, but something inside me clicked. I wanted to live. Long enough to write a news article about how some serial killers did the world a favor. That wasn't what I'd presented to my professor since I'd known it would've been rejected, but it was what I planned to publish. All I'd wanted was to write of my experience and then die by Jack's hand like I should have years ago.

"I can cut you in a deal," Noah said, trying to sound tough, but it just sounded like pleading.

"Oh?" Jack said, curiosity lacing his tone. But I knew better; he was toying with his victim. Nothing more.

Noah slowly got back to his feet, hands raised in the air. "I've got a lot of money. I give you a good cut, and you leave. I forget this happened."

"And what about all your men I killed?" he asked in amusement.

"They can be replaced." Noah turned around, heading toward his desk, but Jack grabbed him from behind.

He pressed his knife against his throat. "What you're going to do is call Jill and tell her she's off the hook for the five thousand dollars."

"You're kidding, right?" When the weapon pressed harder, Noah stuttered as he pulled out his phone. "Whoa. Okay, okay."

My phone rang, and just as I stepped inside the room,

the blade sliced through Noah's flesh. Blood gushed out as Noah pressed his hand against the wound, desperate to stay alive as he gurgled words from his bleeding mouth.

Jack turned toward me, and I froze as he strode forward, bloodied weapon still in his hand. "What are you doing here?" he asked through gritted teeth. "What did you touch?"

"What..." I glanced back at the doors I came through as my heart hammered against my chest. "I touched the doors. Three of them I think..." Fingerprints. "I was here last night. My fingerprints would've been here, anyway."

"Which is why I wiped down the doors when I came inside."

"Shit..." I glanced to his side where Noah laid dead in a pool of his own blood and swallowed hard. "Maybe I can just say I came back to pay the money but walked in on"—I motioned to the room—"this."

"Where's the money, then?" He took a step closer, and this time, I backed away a bit.

"I... Do I have time to go to the bank?"

He scoffed. "The cameras will have you going to the bank after their time of death. No, I have another idea." He walked over to Noah and redialed my number. "Answer it and stay on the line for around a minute."

I did as he said, my hand trembling as I held the phone out in front of me. Silence hung between us as we waited, and finally, after I counted to sixty, I ended the call. He walked over to me as he put away his knife, and I relaxed.

"This is the plan. Listen very carefully and do exactly as I say." He grabbed me by the throat and rammed me against the wall. My body was already sore, and I cried out at the sudden attack.

"That fucking hurts," I spat as my eyes watered from the pain. Asshole knew I was badly beaten. What the hell?

"Language," he hissed before taking one more step toward me, closing the gap between us. "Noah called you, and you didn't answer because you were scared. Second time, you picked up because you were terrified of what he'd do. He offered a deal about your payment, and you agreed to come to the club to talk."

I nodded, wondering where he was going with this. "Okay..."

"Everything was fine when you walked in, but there was no one here, so you went to the back. A fight broke out between Collins' men and another gang. They shot people, and you got stabbed, left for dead by a rookie."

"What—"

Pressure in my left side like a small punch. A tingle spread from the area, intensifying with every second, as though someone was electrocuting me there. Had he tased me? Heat like I'd never felt in my life before throbbed, and I stared down between us. My eyes widened as he pulled back his hand, retracting a small blade with it. I opened and closed my mouth as the pain grew, and I pressed my hand against the wound. Warm liquid soaked through between my fingers, and I let out a cry as I slid down to the floor.

Jack crouched in front of me and pulled off my scarf, pushing it against my wound. "The police are on the way. Someone definitely reported all the shots I fired." His voice was cold and distant—that hurt more than the stab. "I'm giving you the option to walk away now, Jill. If you don't contact me again, I'll never bother you again. If you want out, now's the time to take it." He grasped my chin, forcing me to look into the blackened eyes. "But if you send me any kind of communication, nothing will stop me from keeping you. Do you understand?"

I nodded slowly as black spots filled my vision. He pushed harder against the scarf, and I gasped. "Ow..."

"Put a lot of pressure. It won't be long now, darling girl."

He straightened, and before I could say anything else, he left by a back door. I stayed on the floor, wondering if this plan of his would really work.

32

VICTIM

*N*ina held my hand the entire time I spoke to the detective in charge of this case. Not once did he seem suspicious; if anything, he sounded sorry I was dragged into this whole mess.

"You were so brave," Nina said, giving my fingers a quick squeeze. "You poor thing." She pushed a strand of my hair from my bruised face. "I wish you'd come to me for help."

"I didn't want you to get hurt." That wasn't a lie; even if I could go back in time and change something, I never would've gotten her involved in this mess.

Luckily—or as planned—my stab wound was superficial and only needed a few stitches. They x-rayed me for any broken bones after I told them I'd been beaten, but I was all clear to leave the hospital. Nina drove me home and insisted on coming to visit me during the week to help me with anything I might need. I was thankful, but guilt weighed heavily on me; I'd gotten myself into this mess. And I still didn't know what I wanted to do about Jack. What if it was for the best we went our separate ways? Yet, that thought made my heart ache so hard I thought for sure it would stop.

But what if he'd said that as a kind way of breaking things off with me? Maybe he didn't want me in his life anymore after I'd caused him so much annoyance. I hated my inner thoughts for the constant nagging of what-ifs.

After a week of healing, I was back in class. Elsie nearly broke down when she saw me, and I explained a bit of what had happened. As I'd suspected, she'd assumed I'd left and didn't want her to try and talk me into staying again. She felt beyond guilty, and it took me all of our first class together to convince her I didn't blame her for any of it.

My smartphone dinged with a notification from the professor teaching my next class, stating it would be canceled due to the flu. I checked the time; Jack would be sleeping around this time, but...I had to see him. I knew what it meant, though. That there would be no leaving afterward. Not unless it was by becoming paint for one of his canvases.

I excused myself, stating I was still a bit under the weather, and my professor let me go without any protest. As I went outside into a blast of cold air, I let Nina know my class was canceled but that I would be working on my report for the rest of the day. In a way, I wasn't lying, but there was so much more at stake.

I bounced up and down from one leg to the other, trying to stay warm while doing my best to ignore the constant pain shooting through my body. The taxi took longer to arrive, and by the time it did, I was at risk of becoming an ice sculpture. Thankfully, the vehicle was hot, and I rubbed my hands together as I gave him the address.

Snowflakes fell from the sky, and I leaned my head against the window. What was I going to say to Jack when I got to his place? Should I text him in advance? My heart pounded as I typed in a quick message saying I was on my way to him. That way, if he didn't want to see me, I could save myself a bit of money and go back home already. That thought shattered my heart into a million pieces.

Jack: I'll see you soon.

He didn't refuse—that was already a good sign. But I couldn't guess what his mood was from his text. That made me nervous. I kept glancing from my screen to outside, half-expecting him to suddenly send me a message to go back home instead. By the time the vehicle pulled up to his place, my stomach churned. I paid the driver another forty dollars and slipped out of the car, heading toward Jack's home. Although, I wasn't sure if I should head to the garage or the main door. I wasn't coming in with him this time, nor was I breaking in.

I went to the main door and pressed the button for the doorbell. When Jack opened the door, he moved to the side and motioned me in.

My pulse sped as I entered, slipping off my boots and coat before turning to him.

"So you chose to come back?" he asked in such a stony tone I nearly started crying. "Are you sure this is what you want?"

I nodded as I bit my lower lip. "Is it what you'd like?"

He pulled me in for a hug, holding me close in silence for what felt like an eternity. I didn't mind at all. We belonged together, and I didn't care what it took to stay with him until the end. Until my end.

"Come with me." He led me toward the dining room partition, and my face heated as I remembered how he'd tied me to this table as I tried my best not to bite down into a strawberry while he ate me out.

He sat on one of the chairs, keeping me standing in front of him. "I want to see it."

I already knew what he was talking about; I lifted my top and lowered my leggings a bit so he could see the stitches. They'd have to come out in a little less than a week, but the scarring already looked pretty good.

He traced his finger along it, and I shivered. "I've never seen one of mine stitched up," he said quietly. I couldn't help but grin; it was as though he was talking to someone's pregnant belly.

At the thought, I placed my hand against his, and he looked up at me. "I can't have kids. I had my tubes tied years ago."

He arched an eyebrow as a slow smile curled his lips. "I wouldn't make a good father, so that's good."

I laughed as he went back to the stitches.

"I've never asked to be forgiven for stabbing someone, but I will this time." His brown eyes swam in tears. "Will you forgive me, Jill?"

My heart swelled as I cupped his face. "Of course."

He kissed the scar, then leaned his forehead against my abdomen. "Thank you." He let out a breath, and I smiled. "I'm taking time off starting next week, and I am going to lay low at my cabin while police are investigating the gang murders. Will you come spend Christmas with me?"

I almost squeaked in excitement as I went over what my classes looked like for the next while. "I have a final exam on Friday, but I can leave after." I thought of what this would entail, and a thought crossed my mind. "Is it secluded?"

"It very much is... why?" he asked as though reading my mind.

"Starting on Friday, I want to be hunted like one of

your victims. I want to know what it's like so I can add it to my report."

"On one condition." His gaze darkened, and I swallowed hard. "You understand that what I do to you, I wouldn't do to anyone else."

A shiver shot down my spine as I caught his meaning. I'd be at his mercy. "I accept on the condition you understand I'll do everything in my power to fight you along the way."

His smile widened. "I'm glad to hear it." He got to his feet and leaned into my ear. "I'll see you on Friday, then."

33

GAME

I finished my exam in record time and then headed home. It was already getting dark because of the seasonal time change, and with snow piling on, I gritted my teeth at the inconvenience.

A shadow moved behind me, and I spun around, ready to fight back. Nothing. I was pretty paranoid. Police tape barred my access to the main entrance, and I shivered as I went around toward the parking area instead. What had happened inside my building? My heart raced as I pictured Jack lying on the floor of my apartment, shot dead by the cops. I rushed ahead, but before I got to the entrance, someone grabbed me to the side.

I yelped, but before I could do much more than that, Jack shoved me inside the trunk of his car and closed it. The small space seemed to close in on me, and I pounded against the ceiling with little results.

"I want out!" I screamed as loudly as I could. The car moved forward, and something hit me in the back. I turned around, reaching into my pocket for my phone, but it was gone. Had he taken it, or had I dropped it somewhere?

"Shit... Shit..." I muttered, glancing back and trying to figure out what kept hitting me every time he came to a stop. Finally, after some feeling around, I realized it was the suitcase I'd packed for my two weeks away. He'd likely put police tape there himself, and suddenly, I wanted to be the one to shoot him, the bastard. I hated enclosed places, but I'd never told him that, too scared he'd use it against me at the start. Instead, he'd used it not knowing I was claustrophobic.

The ride took longer than necessary, but without being able to check the time, I didn't know for sure. Maybe it had only been a few minutes, and my mind, in its panic, convinced me it had been hours.

When the car came to a stop, I moved my legs around, ready to kick him in the face and run for it. I'd be giving him a piece of my mind, not caring at all about his no-swearing rules. I had to remember he wasn't the Jack I'd gotten to know anymore; he was going to be himself and hold nothing back. And the thought of that sent excitement through me.

The key unlocked the back, and as soon as the trunk opened, I kicked out. I got him right in the chest, and he staggered back as I jumped out. My legs had gone more numb than I'd thought, and I didn't get far at all before he grabbed me. I landed hard in the snowy driveway and looked around at the forest surrounding us as he straddled my back.

"You fucking son of a bitch. I hate small spaces," I screamed at him while I wriggled.

He tied my wrists together behind my back. "First of all, there's no need to insult my mother," he said with a chuckle. "Second of all, I can't read your mind. And third—"

"Let me guess: *language*."

"Exactly." He pulled me to my feet and led me toward the cutest cabin I'd seen.

It wasn't big the way I'd imagined, but instead, it looked as though it had, at most, one bedroom inside. The rest of the surroundings were nothing but trees; he wasn't kidding when he'd said the place was secluded. Despite the situation, it was peaceful with the falling snow. Even the Christmas lights decorating the small house, as well as a few of the pine trees, gave it such a cozy feel.

I snorted as he led me toward the house, but instead, he continued toward a large shed out back. "I imagine you don't want to get cut, so I suggest you kneel right here and stay still," he said as he pushed me down to my knees in front of the chained door. He unlocked it, and I thought of bolting, but with my hands tied behind my back, I wouldn't get far. The chain fell into the snow with a soft thud, and he slid the doors open. Inside the small area were a bunch of chains and a small cot. It reminded me a lot of the one I'd woken up on when he'd drugged me that first time we officially met; it seemed like a lifetime ago.

He pulled off my coat and threw it to the ground before closing the doors again. The lightbulb hanging overhead was the only illumination inside the place, giving it a creepy feel. As though this was the place where he butchered people.

I asked for this...

A high table on one side of the room caught my attention. He forced me to kneel again before I could see everything on there, but from what I did see, there were a lot of sex toys. I swallowed hard as I looked up at him.

"Is this something you usually do?" I already knew the

answer was no, but I needed to hear him say it.

"No. I bought these a few days ago. Needed to prepare for your big day today." He put a collar around my neck, and I shivered when the sound of a click locked it onto me. "Since this is what you wanted so much."

He grabbed a small chain and hooked it to the collar before locking the other end onto a metal hook embedded into the floor; I hadn't even noticed the thing next to my knee. At this angle, I couldn't get up even if I wanted to, and suddenly, the ground was too cold through my leggings.

"Why did you want to play the victim?" he asked, sliding out his knife and pointing it at me.

"I want to add it to my report." It wasn't a lie, but it wasn't the full truth of it either.

"You're hiding something, and until you tell me the whole reason, well..." He left the rest hanging as he stood. He walked around me, and I yelped when he grabbed my ass and lifted me to my feet. I was forced to lean forward with only his hands keeping me from falling flat on my face. He ripped off my leggings and panties, and my body heated at the action. But he didn't touch me beyond that, instead forcing me back down to kneel. This time, the ground was way too cold against my skin, and I shivered.

There was a loud click, and I glanced back as he moved a portable heater behind me. "This will keep you warm. Wouldn't want you to catch a cold, now would we?" he said with a wink.

I wanted to call him every name in the book, but before I could, he grabbed the hem of my top and wrenched. It ripped, the sound resonating through the small room.

"You fucking bastard. What the fuck?" I yelled at him. I liked that top.

He just chuckled as he yanked it off of me, then proceeded to take my bra off next. Thankfully, the straps were detachable, so he didn't need to ruin it. I was still fuming.

"I've been meaning to do this for some time..." He went back to the high table and dangled something in front of me. A ball gag, but instead of the gag, it was a bar of soap.

I gawked at him. "You wouldn't..." But I knew all too well he very much would.

I pressed my lips together when he walked around me again, but he pinched my nose. As I did my best to only suck in a few breaths here and there, he was eventually able to shove the bar between my teeth. He strapped the leather bounds together at the back of my head, and I grimaced as the taste filled my mouth. I would murder him for this.

He grabbed something else but didn't show it to me. It was made of cloth with buckles on the side, kind of like a pair of panties that detached on the sides. "I'm sure you'll enjoy this," he said with amusement as he slipped it under me between my legs. I pushed my knees together, stopping him from being able to continue. He stared at me for a few seconds before reaching behind him and pulling out a riding crop. Without a word, he slammed it down against my upper thigh, and a muffled scream left me. The soap tasted stronger as I bit into it, saliva dribbling down the corners of my mouth.

Fuck. You.

However, I parted my knees again, not wanting to feel that kind of sting again. My body had healed from the beating I'd gotten a few weeks back, and I wasn't planning on having that many more bruises. Although I couldn't deny this wasn't the same thing at all; the way Jack took control in this situation, his calm demure, really turned me on.

As he put the crop away, he pulled out nipple clamps, and my heart skipped a beat. I'd never had those used on me before, but I was excited to see how they'd feel. He took a sip from the paper cup on the table, then leaned forward to suckle one of my nipples in his mouth. I gasped; whatever he'd drunk was icy cold, and my hard peaks stiffened even more.

He pulled away and then clamped it, adjusting the tightness with care. A slow throb turned into pressure between my legs, and I breathed a bit faster. He did the same thing to my other nipple, and by the time he finished, I was panting. Heat pooled from my pussy, and I nearly bit down against the soap again.

"You enjoy that, don't you?" he said with amusement as he gave the small chain connecting the clamps together a small tug.

I moaned, arching back, throbbing with more need than I'd thought possible. He grabbed the strange underwear, and a strangled sound left my throat as he pushed something big against my wet opening. He thrust the dildo inside me, and I groaned against the building pressure. Something hard pressed against my clit, and I whimpered as it vibrated to life.

Oh...they were that kind of panties.

I'd only ever seen these in pornos, and although I'd been curious to try, I never thought I'd be doing it while chained to the ground of a shed as a bar of soap assaulted my tongue.

He slid the doors open and glanced over his shoulder at me with an icier smile than the weather. "Enjoy yourself for a while." They shut again, and I let out a growl as I throbbed with release.

34

DARK SIDE

y the time Jack came back for me, it had stopped snowing. I was sore from being stuck in the same position. On top of that, I'd cum several times from the clit stimulation and was oversensitive to even the smallest movement. As soon as he turned off the vibrator, I nearly cried in relief.

He covered me in a blanket before picking me up in his arms and carrying me out. I winced in the cold, but within a few steps, he was already inside the cabin. It was a one-room design with a tiny kitchen on one side and a small living room with a large fireplace on the other. Flames roared inside the pit as though it had been lit for quite some time, and I relaxed as the heat enveloped me.

Placing me on the loveseat, he unbound my arms, massaging each one thoroughly as he flexed them to the front. I whimpered at the sudden opposite movements, but as the minutes ticked on, my limbs felt better and better. He continued kneading my muscles as he undid the gag, and I spit out the bar of soap; never in my life had I hated something so much.

He pushed my hair to the side, and I let out a breath as his lips brushed against the crook of my neck. "How are you feeling?" he asked in a hushed tone.

I opened my mouth to say something but closed it again when no words came to mind. He'd locked me away in a shed for God knows how long. All the while overstimulating me while I was alone. Tears rolled down my face as he reached around me and undid the nipple clamps. A rush of blood prickled against them, and I hissed through my teeth at the sudden warmth.

He stood and helped me to my feet, his eyes darkening as he stared at me. Without a word, he helped me out of the underwear and then covered me with the blanket again. I was about to ask him if I could go to sleep, but he picked me up again and sat back down with me between his legs. He held me close, and I leaned my face against his chest, listening to his heart beating.

"I didn't like being left alone," I said in a cracking voice.

"Then I won't leave you alone anymore." He kissed the top of my head. "Anything else?"

I thought back for a second. "It was hot... ripping my top off, but I really liked that one."

"I'll buy you a new one, but from now on, I'll make sure you're wearing something you don't like before I destroy any of your things."

"Thanks," I said quietly as I closed my eyes. "Maybe tomorrow we could decorate your Christmas tree..."

The crackling of the fire lulled me to sleep, but it wasn't deep.

"Let's go to bed," he whispered as he pulled me up.

I trudged along, following him without much thought. I was still sore, but I was getting better by the second; being able to communicate what I liked and didn't was somehow so freeing.

The room was small, with the queen bed taking up most of the space. A dresser stood facing it, but apart from that, the room was bare. He placed me onto the bed, and the mattress dipped beneath me. I wrapped the blanket tighter against myself as he moved to the dresser and began undressing. My pulse quickened, my body thrumming with anticipation, yet at the same time, I was so overwhelmed with what I'd just been through I couldn't imagine being intimate in that moment.

Before I could put my thoughts into words, he returned to the bed and pulled back the blankets. "You're going to freeze."

I slipped beneath them as he did, lying down next to me. He pulled me close, and I rested my head against his chest.

"You're not treating me like a victim anymore?" I asked quietly.

"I don't want to... Besides, I think you just want to see my dark side." He traced his finger along my jaw. "There's more than one way to see that side of me."

I had to admit he was right; I wanted to see that part of him. So I could maybe describe what his victims saw before they died. But he was different with me. Didn't enjoy it like he did with others. He was so warm, and the rhythm of his heart rocked me to sleep.

Moonlight filtered through the curtains, and I frowned when I realized I was alone in bed. I swung my legs to the side, tightening the blanket around myself as I went to the window. The Christmas lights outside glowed in different colors, some buried beneath the freshly fallen snow.

Jack approached the cabin, dragging a small pine tree behind him. I stared at him, my chest squeezing; he didn't have a Christmas tree until just then. Was it because I'd mentioned decorating one tomorrow? He vanished around the house, and I made my way into the living room. The door opened, and he dragged the tree inside.

"What time is it?" I asked as he closed the door behind him.

"Very early," he said with a chuckle. "You should go back to sleep."

I motioned at the tree. "Do you need any help?"

"We'll put it up tomorrow like you said." He leaned the tree against the wall, then slipped off his coat and boots.

I approached him, reaching up toward his hair and brushing off the snowflakes. "You need to get warmed up," I whispered as I dropped the blanket, leaving me naked.

I led him to the loveseat, and when he sat down, I straddled his lap. My heart pounded against my chest as I leaned down and kissed him. He pulled off his t-shirt, and I ran my hands along his chest.

"Thank you for the tree," I said with a smile.

"You know you don't have to have sex with me to thank me for something." He looked concerned for a second before I shook my head.

"I need to be close to you right now." I undid his pants and giggled as he held on to me with one hand while pushing them down the rest of the way.

When we were both naked, I grasped his erection and lifted myself onto my knees. His cock pulsated against my wet opening, and I slowly lowered myself down, one delicious inch at a time. I dug my fingers into his shoulders as I rode him, his shaft filling me up to the hilt. Our breathing was hard and fast as he cupped my breasts in each hand, fondling them. He slid his arms around me, straightening as he held me closer to him. My nipples brushed against his chest, hardening them under the rubbing of our skin. God, he felt so good.

He held me still in his arms, then pounded into me hard. I arched back, and he grabbed my throat, squeezing until the air left my lungs. Pressure grew from between my legs, and my eyes widened as a wave of orgasms crashed against me. The sound of his cock pumping into my wetness filled the room, and I came over and over. He stiffened for a second, then shook violently as he released himself inside of me.

I let myself fall against him, holding each other as we both breathed unevenly through small gasps. I wasn't sure how long we stayed that way, but by the time he got to his feet, carrying me with him, I was already half asleep. Safe in his arms.

35

THE TRUTH

The shopping cart kept jamming, and I kicked it.

"That's not very festive," Jack said with a grin as he grabbed a tree stand.

"I'll wish it Merry Christmas when I do it next time." I scanned the shelves. "What did you ask Santa for this year?" I asked with a wink.

"You."

My face heated, and I busied myself with a few mugs; they were suddenly so interesting. "Well, considering you've been naughty, I'm guessing you'll get coal."

He leaned toward my ear. "Maybe I could draw on your naked body with it."

I pushed him away with a giggle, trying my best not to combust into flames. He hadn't said it loudly at all, but in public, he might as well have shouted it.

I grabbed a cylinder of bobbles, turning it side to side so it would sparkle in the light. "How about these?"

"I love the way you handle balls," he muttered.

I whacked him with the cylinder, convinced I was

redder than most of the decorations around us. "You stop that right now, or I'll—"

"What?" he asked, pulling me closer to him as he chuckled. "Since when are you so shy?"

"Since there are other people around us," I hissed, but I couldn't help but laugh.

"Hardly." He motioned at the empty aisle we stood in. "There are maybe four other people in this place, and most of them are already paying for their things near the entrance."

I put the bobbles into the cart, then stared at the lights. "You like the different colored ones?"

"Do you?" he asked as he grabbed a box. When I nodded, he put it in next to the cylinder. "Then those are the ones I want."

After our quick shopping trip in the nearest town, we put up the tree together while Christmas music played in the background. I couldn't believe I was spending the holidays with Jack after everything; it all was so surreal. It was forever ago I spent time with someone who felt like family.

At the thought, my chest squeezed, but I pushed away at the unease. Part of me didn't know if I wanted to go through with my plan anymore. But it had been in place for so long, I didn't know a life outside it anymore.

He returned from our room with a black binder and handed it to me without a word. I arched an eyebrow as I took it, my heart pounding in my chest as I opened it.

Inside was a card collection of different kinds of jacks, all with a bloody fingerprint on the corners and names written on the cards. My pulse throbbed in my ears as my mouth opened, and I realized what this was: his trophies. I flipped through them, trying to do the calculations in my mind. There were at least a hundred.

"How did you get all their names?" I asked quietly.

"Checked their wallets for IDs. If there weren't any, I put down John or Jane Doe."

I stopped on a page, recognizing my foster parents' names. Side by side. One drowned, the other choked to death.

"Do you mind if I take down some notes real quick?"

He nodded, and I rushed to my suitcase, pulling out my notebook. It wasn't long before I was scribbling down what I saw inside the binder—obviously without mentioning any names. Before I knew it, I had everything I'd ever wanted for my report and more.

I bit my lower lip as I put my notebook aside and pulled the binder back. "You asked if I had a good childhood. I didn't lie when I said it was filled with love, but..." I let out a shuddering breath, unable to meet his gaze. "My aunt passed away from cancer when I was thirteen years old. There was no other family who could take me in, so I ended up in foster care."

"I see..." His tone was unreadable, so I looked up at him. Darkness lingered in his gaze. "I'm sorry that happened to you."

"I didn't lie, but I know that's a technicality to say my adolescence wasn't great. And I'm sorry I lied." I stared back down at the names swimming in front of my eyes. "My foster parents were... very abusive. Melanie belittled and beat me often, and Don... he forced himself on me more than once."

His hands curled into fists as he slid closer to me on the loveseat. I forced a smile as I pointed at both names. "And you don't have to threaten to kill them because you already did. Twelve years ago."

He froze, staring at me as though he was suddenly seeing a ghost.

"I was suicidal by the time I was fifteen years old. I

wanted everything to end. For the pain to stop. And one night, someone broke into our RV, and I hid in the closet..." I held his gaze this time. "I watched as you killed them both and became my hero. The one who saved me from suffering."

"That's how you knew about the cards..." he said in barely a whisper.

I nodded. "And now I've got the final piece." I raised the binder. "I can finally finish my report on why some serial killers are important to the world. Because people fall through cracks, and sometimes, it takes a murder to get rid of evil people."

He cupped my face. "I didn't rescue you, Jill. You did that by yourself. I may have expedited the process, but you would've gotten out. I know you would. You're stronger than you realize and much braver, too."

"We'll see if you still think that of me by the time I'm finished writing the report," I said with a forced smile. I placed my hand against his. "One way or another, you did rescue me. From myself, at least. Thank you."

I got to my feet and paced. The freezing weather suddenly was warm in comparison to what I felt like inside. I needed to tell him the whole truth.

I pulled out the card I'd picked—the jack of spades—and handed it to him. He stared at it, then back to me with a frown.

"That's the final part of my plan. To die the way I was supposed to all those years ago." I took a step closer. "You don't leave witnesses, and the only reason I survived was because you didn't know I was there." My throat tightened. I couldn't seem to breathe properly. "So I chose this one, and now it's... time."

He ripped up the card and let the pieces drop to the floor. I was about to protest, but he pointed at the side of my abdomen. "I already stabbed you. That card was done."

"Then I want to pick another one. Or you choose with the joker." I was sounding hysterical even to my own ears. Why wouldn't he kill me so I could finally end this plan?

"Fine." The word sliced through the air like a knife as he pulled out a deck of cards and opened it. He handed me the first card—a joker—and I took it. "The way you die is of old age with me."

"What—"

"You heard me." He cupped my face in his hands. "You're stuck with me until you die of natural causes."

I gawked at him, eyes wide.

"I've picked for you, and now you choose my fate."

I pulled the second card—the second joker—and smiled. "Same for you."

EPILOGUE
ASK

I sat at the rounded table, running my hand along the white tablecloth. A chandelier hung in the middle of the open room, and I smiled as Jack looked over the menu.

My final report sat, forgotten, on my laptop, forever commemorating what I'd learned about the serial killer, but now, I was getting to know the man. And I loved him more every day. To my surprise, he didn't kill as much; when I mentioned that, he laughed and said he was thinking of retiring. Said he didn't need it anymore.

I sipped on the rosé I'd ordered as he put down the fancy menu and stared at me. His gaze burned with something I couldn't put my finger on, as though he was trying to look into my very soul.

"I have one last ask of you, Jill," he said quietly as he reached into his jacket pocket.

The world seemed to vanish around us as he got onto one knee and pulled out a small black box. He opened it, and a beautiful diamond ring sparkled from within.

"Will you marry me?" he asked in a hushed tone.

I flung my arms around his neck, laughing and crying. "Yes!"

He pulled me back, smiling as he slipped the ring onto my finger. "I love you, darling girl."

"I love you too," I said, beaming as I hugged him close again.

That unspoken final ask was more than just marrying him; it was about living and growing old together.

ABOUT THE AUTHOR

M. A. Fréchette writes the darker side of romance.

Being an extremist, she loves both the dark aspects of life and everything sweet. All her stories are either set in Canada where she lives or in alternate worlds she made up while living within her imagination. When not writing, she thinks of the next scene or plot while enjoying video games. Although she has a fascination for monsters, with a bachelor degree in criminology, she understands there's no need to create the paranormal; humans are capable of inflicting nightmares of their own.

Please feel free to reach out through any social media. I truly love hearing from readers!

 facebook.com/AuthorMAF

 twitter.com/authormaf

 instagram.com/authormaf

 amazon.com/author/authormaf

 bookbub.com/authors/m-a-frechette

ALSO BY M. A. FRÉCHETTE

A Demon's Love series

MY SOUL TO GIVE (book #1)

MY LIFE TO TAKE (book #2)

Unbroken series

A THOUSAND WORDS (book #1)